FLIPPING FOR HIM

A GAY YA ROMANCE

JEFF ADAMS

BIG GAY
Media

FLIPPING
for HIM

JEFF ADAMS

FLIPPING FOR HIM

Finding a guy was easy. Keeping him might be harder than running up a tree.

Kevin McCollum is a high school junior with the usual things on his mind: getting good grades, having fun, and finding a boyfriend. The last one always eluded him until he noticed the "parkour guy." After several days of pretending to study while watching the attractive teen jump on rocks, run up trees, and do flips, Shin finally comes over to introduce himself. As they start dating, Kevin should've known it wouldn't be that easy.

Shin's parents only want their son to date Japanese boys. When cultures clash and pressures mount, Kevin has no idea how to subvert traditions and Shin's parents to keep the boy he cares about.

Kevin will need to clear some tricky obstacles to make his modern love story a reality.

Flipping for Him
Copyright © 2015 by Jeff Adams
All rights reserved.

Cover design: Sylvia Frost, sfrostcovers.com

ONE

KEVIN ENJOYED CUTTING through Central Park on his way home
from school in the afternoons. Usually he'd go through at 72nd Street
traveling east to west, taking a direct route if he was in a hurry or
going downstairs by Bethesda Fountain if he had some time to kill.

Since it was a warm, sunny day he took the fountain route and
then cut north around the lake. It was a spectacular day for early
March and despite being a weekday afternoon, plenty of folks were
out taking advantage of the nice weather. Kevin went past the lake
into a clearing lined with trees and scattered with several clusters of
rocks. This was one of his favorite spots in the city because it had a
great view of the residential buildings lining Central Park West,
featuring some exceptional architecture. Sometimes he would sketch
nearby buildings, as the clearing got great light on sunny days.

Today he only had one thing on his mind. Warming himself in
the sun.

Kevin craved the heat, as his thin frame was easily chilled. He
didn't look emaciated, but at six-two and one hundred-eighty pounds
he was certainly lanky. His metabolism burned up food so quickly
that his weight hadn't fluctuated more than five pounds since his

growth spurt at fourteen. Now sixteen, he had a thin but okay body. While it would've been easy to add some definition by hitting the weights, he preferred running over going to the gym.

Running was his first love. Track caught his eye while watching the summer Olympics when he was ten. Seeing those guys tear through the hundred meters with tremendous bursts of speed was thrilling. They reminded him of the Flash, and what ten-year-old doesn't want to be a superhero? Kevin had the same red hair as the comic book hero, so he sort of looked the part, too. Running was also how he fell in love with the park. He lived only a few blocks away, and would often take a morning run around one of the loops.

Kevin wasn't alone. Several others had the same idea, and were lying in the grass or on the rocks. It wasn't surprising since it was the first decent spring-like day after the deep-freeze of winter. He hopped up onto his favorite boulder. It was big enough so that when he laid down his feet wouldn't hang off the edge. He put his hands on the surface of the stone and felt the warmth. He removed the blue school blazer, folded it and placed it in his backpack. He did the same with his white button-down shirt. After wearing multiple layers for the past five months, he was glad to be out of them and enjoying the sun.

He stretched out, closed his eyes and listened to the park. Birds chirped, no doubt thrilled at the sudden turn of the weather as well. Kids laughed and played in the distance. Periodically, the crack of a softball against a bat came from the nearby ballfields.

Despite the welcome sounds of spring, Kevin was preoccupied. He needed to get busy on the big college hunt. The guidance counselors were bugging him about picking colleges since he was well into the second half of his junior year. Even his parents had brought it up recently. He wanted to stay in the city and was hopeful NYU would take him. He had solid grades, decent extracurriculars and expected high SAT scores.

Nevertheless, NYU wasn't a sure thing. Competition was fierce.

He needed to have backup options that had the drawing and architecture programs he wanted.

His mind drifted, and, as it usually did, it settled on Javier. He'd met Javier the first day of their sophomore year. His jet black hair, bushy eyebrows and dark brown eyes had caught Kevin's attention immediately. His thick legs from playing soccer didn't hurt either. He also packed a lot of muscle into his five-six frame, and the way the regulation button-down hung off his built chest drove Kevin wild. Kevin dreamed about his pecs and longed to get him out of that shirt. Kevin even considered joining the soccer team as a way to see more of Javier.

Fortunately they shared three classes so they were around each other a lot. Four weeks into the semester, Kevin missed a day of school coming back late from a trip and used that opportunity to ask Javier about missed notes and assignments. That started a friendship. Several pings on his gaydar later, Kevin took the leap and asked Javier on a date.

Javier's "hell yeah" thrilled Kevin and just like that they were couple. It wasn't long after the first date that Kevin got Javier out of his shirt—and everything else—to mess around. For both of them it was the first time, but they quickly figured out what they liked.

Unfortunately, Javier moved away this past summer, just two weeks before junior year began. They knew the move was coming at the end of June because Javier's father accepted a transfer to Seattle. It was a crazy ten weeks between the announcement and the move as Kevin and Javier spent every hour they could together. Kevin considered himself lucky that Javier remained a friend.

The sun felt good beating down on Kevin's chest as the warm rock heated up his back. He opened an eye to check his watch. He'd been lying here for almost fifteen minutes. Being fair-skinned, he sat up, crossed his legs under himself and pulled his shirt back on. He left it unbuttoned, but he covered his back and arms and adjusted so the sun was behind him. The last thing he wanted was to burn.

Looking across the grass, Kevin saw a guy jumping, almost bouncing, around on some rocks. He jumped from the ground up onto a rock and then jumped quickly from rock to rock. If the next boulder was too far away, he'd hit the ground, and do a few flips until he was close enough to jump up onto another one. After jumping around a bit more, he ran towards a tree where he grabbed a low branch and pushed off the trunk with his feet. Once he was away from the tree, he released the limb and tried to do a flip to land on his feet. Unfortunately, he hit the ground before the flip was complete. He ended up on his side, landing hard.

That had to hurt.

The guy didn't seem to care. He quickly jumped up, charged at another tree and ran about half way up before he tried a backflip. He ended up on the ground again, just like the first time. He'd tweaked his technique a bit, but the result was the same.

Kevin knew about parkour and loved watching it on TV. He thought it might be cool to try out for one of those shows, but he had no idea how to train for it. And he'd never seen anyone do it in person. Until now.

This guy was pretty good, too.

Kevin seemed to be the only one paying attention, which was a shame since the guy was putting on quite a show. He must've been practicing a particular routine because he kept doing it, even though the final move kept crashing him to the ground.

From Kevin's perspective, it looked like the guy wasn't getting enough height off the ground to be able to finish the flip. Clearly he could do flips. This one was just not quite working yet. The tenacity was impressive, and finally paid off as he did the swing, pushed off from the tree, flipped and landed on his feet. It wasn't a perfect landing, but it was a landing rather than a crash. The guy let out a whoop of excitement. Kevin grinned. He was thrilled for the guy, and psyched he'd seen it happen.

The guy stripped out of his shirt and wiped the sweat from his brow. Kevin had been so busy watching him execute his moves that he hadn't really paid attention to what he looked like.

The guy was hot.

His thick black hair, styled just a bit, reminded Kevin of Javier. His chest, shoulders and abs were chiseled and he imagined they'd be rock hard to the touch. Kevin thought that Javier had been ripped, but this guy went beyond that. His body was smooth. While he usually liked guys with some hair, every now and then a smooth guy caught Kevin's eye.

The guy trotted over to a backpack leaning against a nearby tree. Kevin couldn't keep his eyes off him as he put his t-shirt in the bag and pulled out a bottle of water. Watching him lift the bottle to his lips, with the small flex in his arm and the glimpse of dark hair under his armpit made Kevin catch his breath. He hadn't felt like this in months.

Kevin's phone rang, pulling him out of his trance. He slid down the rock and pulled his phone from his pack.

"Marshall," he said as he picked up the call, "what's goin' on man?"

"Not much," Kevin's best friend said. "Just got home, stopped by your place but you weren't there yet. Wanna hit the first show of *X-Men* tonight with some of the guys?"

"Yeah, man. Where and when?"

Marshall rattled off the details. They were headed to Kevin's favorite theatre in Chelsea where the popcorn was always fresh and the seats comfortable. He'd have to get home and blaze through some homework so he'd be done before showtime. Tomorrow might be rough since there wouldn't be much sleep tonight, but it was worth it to see this movie early. At least he hoped it would be. You could never be too sure with movies these days.

"Cool," Kevin said. "I'll buy the ticket now. Stop by my place when you head out."

"Will do. Later, Kev."

Kevin ended the call and looked up to see the runner moving through another rotation of the same sequence. He nailed the difficult flip again. Kevin smiled, glad to see the guy's confidence grow.

He'd only been watching for, at most, twenty minutes but there was already great improvement in the technique.

Kevin quickly used his phone to buy a ticket so he wouldn't have to worry about the theater selling out. It only took a minute, but when he looked back to the rocks, the guy was gone.

"Damnit," Kevin muttered to himself.

Kevin was disappointed, but he didn't have time to linger. He buttoned up his shirt and grabbed his pack. Taking off towards his place on 76th Street, he tried to keep an eye out for the guy. If he ever saw him again, Kevin resolved to tell him how much he enjoyed watching his moves.

TWO

"Where are we going?" Marshall asked as he walked with Kevin through the park after school. They rarely finished school at the same time but when they did they usually walked home together.

"I thought we'd cut through the park here. It's a nice day, so why not?"

"Um, okay. But I thought we were going to get meatballs, which is south and you're taking us north."

Kevin considered this. It'd been almost a week since he'd been back to the spot where he'd seen parkour guy--yes, that was the name Kevin bestowed on him--do his routine. Between study group, homework and a couple of rainy days, there'd been no time.

"I need to see something," he said, nonchalantly as they rounded the lake. "It'll only take a second."

If the guy was there, he'd want to stay much longer than that, and he'd have to figure out a way to stall Marshall, which wouldn't be easy.

Marshall was as straight as they come, and while Kevin had done a fine job serving as his wingman, as evidenced by an upcoming first date with Cassie, Marshall was not as adept at playing that role for

Kevin. In the time since Javier left, Marshall had tried to point out guys he thought Kevin might be interested in. It was amusing that this big football linebacker, so large Kevin could almost hide behind him, was trying to play matchmaker for his gay best friend. Kevin appreciated the effort, though the results were often mixed.

As soon as they cleared the trees, Kevin realized their little side trip would be brief. Parkour guy wasn't there. Instead, a couple kids jumped and played on the rocks where Kevin first saw him. Kevin glanced at his watch. He knew it was a long shot but had hoped the guy would be out practicing around the same time as before. But no such luck.

"Okay, I'm good. Let's go."

Kevin spun around and headed back in the direction they'd come.

"That's it?" Marshall asked as he caught up with Kevin. "We didn't even stop."

"I told you, it'd only be a second."

"Sometimes you're weird."

"This coming from the guy who'll go eight blocks out of his way for meatballs."

"That's different. That's food. Plus, I know exactly where the meatball truck is. We just went to some random spot in the park and that was it."

"But you..." Kevin stopped in his tracks.

Parkour guy was walking towards them. He wore sweat pants and a long sleeve workout shirt this time, but Kevin recognized him immediately. The muscles that teased from afar, where eye-poppingly impressive at close range under the tight shirt. The biceps and pecs pulled the fabric taut. Kevin wanted to run his hands all over him.

"What the hell, Kev?" Marshall asked as he bumped into Kevin just as parkour guy passed them, nodding and smiling. Kevin wondered if that smile was for him. He couldn't tell.

Up close the guy looked incredible. Everything about him

exuded self-confidence, without a trace of arrogance, and his gate was comfortable and easy. Kevin turned as parkour guy passed and let his eyes drift down to his butt, admiring how perfect it looked.

"Oh shit," Marshall said through a laugh, "you're completely into that guy."

Kevin thrust an elbow into Marshall's stomach to shut him up.

"You don't need to tell the whole park," Kevin said without looking at his friend.

If parkour guy heard Marshall he didn't let on. Kevin watched him go over to the rocks and drop his pack in the same spot. One of the kids who'd been climbing came over and bumped fists with him. Clearly a sign that this was parkour guy's spot.

The two boys and one girl gathered around and parkour guy talked to them as he went through some stretches. It was obvious they all knew each other. Kevin guessed the kids were around ten years old. He was impressed that parkour guy interacted with them so easily while most guys his age could not. Even Kevin would've been uncomfortable.

"So you drug me over here to watch a guy do some stretches?"

"What if I did? I've stalked girls with you," Kevin said while keeping his eyes locked on parkour guy.

"True. But I'm usually more of a chaser than you are. In fact, I don't think I've seen you take this much interest in a guy in a while, probably since Javier."

"It takes the right guy to get my attention."

Parkour guy started his warm up by making some easy jumps between the rocks. His young audience sat at a distance, safely out of his way.

"Why are they watching him jump on rocks?" Marshall sounded incredulous as he moved to stand next to Kevin. "For that matter, why are *you* watching him jump on rocks?"

"You'll see. Give it a minute."

As soon as Kevin said it, parkour guy did his first trick, executing two flips between rocks. He sped up as he found the rhythm Kevin recognized from last time. There were new moves, too, as he did a series of backflips to launch himself on to some of the rocks that were closer to the ground. Then he made a run for the tree. Kevin caught his breath, knowing what was about to happen. Parkour guy scaled the base of the tree, grabbed the branch and pushed hard and away, arcing into a perfect flip before nailing the landing. Kevin smiled.

The junior audience applauded. Parkour guy turned and gave a small bow.

"Damn," Marshall said in sort of a whisper of reverence. "I didn't know real people did that."

"Right?" Kevin looked at Marshall for the first time since parkour guy showed up. "See why I'm interested?"

"I do. Though if I saw a girl do that, I'd be so intimidated. Not sure I could compete with that."

"You? The big, bad football player, would be afraid of an athletic girl?"

"Hell yeah. And he's more than just athletic. I'm good with the forward momentum, but once you start doing flips and shit, that's more badass than anything I've got."

"Think how limber she'd be though. All the different moves she could put on you."

Marshall thought about it for a moment, and then slowly stared to smile. "Hmmmmm. Hadn't thought about that."

"Uh-huh. Believe me, I've thought in vivid detail about what he and I could do."

Kevin watched parkour guy continue his workout.

"Is this a real crush or just a jerk off fantasy?"

"It's definitely in the fantasy category right now. Not sure I've got the balls to do anything else with it."

Kevin watched as parkour guy flipped off the tree one more time.

"He seems like a nice guy, or at least he's good with those kids," Marshall said. "That's a good sign, right? And since when don't you have the balls to do something?"

"I don't know. I feel like he's out of my league."

"Why? You're both athletes. Seems like he's got a good personality."

Marshall said this as parkour guy called the kids closer to chat.

"The only thing you don't know is if he's into guys. Or is your gaydar pinging?"

Kevin's gaydar was pretty good, but not infallible. "I have no idea. I don't have enough to go on. What do you think?"

Parkour guy offered a hand up to one of the boys and led him to a rock. There was a demonstration—a very slow run up to the rock, where parkour guy planted his feet and executed a front flip, landing softly in the grass. The boy watched intently as he executed the move twice more, increasing the speed and momentum each time.

"No idea," Marshall finally said.

After the demo, parkour guy squatted down and talked to the boy at his level for a bit before standing up and tussling his hair.

The boy went to where parkour guy had stood moments before. He got into a run-ready pose, nodding his head as parkour guy continued to give him instructions. Instead of taking off fast, the boy and parkour guy moved together, slowly, side-by-side, towards the rock. The surprising thing was that as the boy approached the rock, parkour guy got down next to the rock and allowed the boy to flip over his arm. Parkour guy looked completely in control of the flip and the boy planted his feet firmly on the grass.

Kevin and Marshall heard the boy's excited laughter as he high-fived his teacher. The other kids clapped and cheered enthusiastically.

"Like I said," Marshall continued, "he seems like a good guy."

Kevin watched in amazement as each kid went through the same moves, flipping off the rock with parkour guy's help. Kevin wanted to join in.

"So you gonna talk to him or not?"

"Not today," Kevin said, a hint of disappointment in his voice. "We've got places to go and I don't have the right words today. Plus I don't want you to be around when I do it. I don't want any witnesses if I crash and burn."

Marshall opened his mouth to speak, but Kevin cut him off.

"I know you wouldn't give me grief, but I'd still rather die of embarrassment on my own." Marshall nodded and didn't offer further resistance. "Let's get going."

"Yeah, I've seen enough of your drooling for today."

Marshall gave Kevin a playful punch in the shoulder.

As they walked away, Kevin turned back for one last look. The kids were gone and parkour guy was drinking some water.

"I just need to figure out what I'm going to say," Kevin said.

"It shouldn't be too hard. Maybe ask him about parkour. You like the sport. You've wanted to try it. If nothing else you might end up with a friend who can coach you."

Kevin looked over at his wingman, smiling. "I just might do it," he said, determination seeping into his voice.

"I guess I know where you'll be after school the next few days."

"Yeah, probably. Too pathetic?"

"Nah," Marshall said. "It only gets pathetic if you don't meet him. Then you become a stalker."

THREE

Kevin made sure to drop by the place he now referred to as "parkour point" every day on his way home. On warmer days he'd hang out on a rock with a good view and study. Other days he would just walk by without stopping. Every day parkour guy, or P.G. for short, was there. Most days P.G. was alone going through his routine, which was getting longer and more intricate. Sometimes the trio of kids were hanging out, too.

Kevin liked that P.G. always had time for the kids. He wondered what would happen if he went over and sat down with them to watch. Kevin didn't have the nerve to do that, but he thought about it. He wasn't sure of himself in this situation. With Javier it'd been different. He had a reason to go up and introduce himself, but with P.G. he had nothing. If he approached him now, he was afraid he'd turn into a babbling mess.

Kevin came back to what Marshall had said before—at some point, he was simply going to become a stalker.

It was an especially warm day when Kevin arrived at parkour point. A dozen or so guys were scattered across the lawn, their shirts open, enjoying the weather. Normally, Kevin took in the display, but his attention was focused elsewhere. Across the way, P.G. was going through his routine, already shirtless and wearing shorts instead of the usual sweatpants.

Now almost every muscle was on display and it was a lot to take in. The guy was beyond hot. Kevin had never seen someone around his age as well defined as P.G., not even the athletes. He'd seen the pecs and abs before. But seeing the legs now, it was as if someone had sculpted Kevin's perfect guy.

Kevin composed himself and sat down on his rock. He pulled out the chem book hoping that doing homework would reduce his stalker quotient. He also unbuttoned his shirt because he didn't want to miss out on some sun.

Over the next half hour or so, Kevin did his best to look like he was studying while often looking beyond his book to P.G. The routine seemed to be getting more elaborate, and more effortless, all the time. He enjoyed watching P.G., but didn't know for certain whether the routine was good or not, or if the moves were being executed as intended. But it didn't matter. Kevin thought every move was perfect.

After a while, Kevin put his book down and reached into his backpack for some water. When he looked up, P.G. was gone. How did that happen? He was there one minute and then gone the next! Usually it took some time for P.G. to put on his shirt and collect his things, but not this time. Had Kevin been reading so long that he missed it? That didn't seem possible, yet there was no sign of him.

"Oh well," he said to no one. There'd be more days to watch, and to watch him in just the shorts since it would only be getting warmer from here on out. Kevin refocused on the chem book. Even though P.G. was gone, there was no reason to take his studying inside.

"Hi."

Kevin jumped as the voice came from just behind him. He turned and found P.G. standing right behind him, close enough to touch. His shirt was on, but he was still in shorts showing off his muscled legs, glistening with sweat. His backpack was slung over one shoulder and the water bottle was in his hand.

Kevin stared a bit too long before he spoke.

"Um. Hi. Hello."

"I thought I'd come over since I see you here all the time, sometimes watching me." His voice shifted into something between sexy and flirty. Kevin already loved the sound of his voice. "Sometimes trying not to watch me, but watching anyway."

P.G. smiled, staring right at Kevin.

"Um. Well. Yeah. You caught me." Kevin smiled back nervously, a little embarrassed that he'd been discovered.

"I'm Shin."

Suddenly P.G. had a name. Shin reached out a hand, which Kevin took. Shin's handshake was firm.

"I'm Kevin."

"Nice to meet you," said Shin. "So, you enjoy the show?"

"Yeah," Kevin said loudly, and perhaps a little too quickly. Fearing he sounded too excited, he toned it down, trying to play it cool. "Um. I mean... sure. It's cool stuff all the flips, turns and jumps. I've seen it on TV, but never up close like this."

Kevin tried to stay focused on Shin's eyes, which were a gorgeous dark brown with some lighter highlights, but he wasn't entirely successful. His eyes kept drifting down as they talked, drinking him in at close range.

"You could come closer you know? You've seen me with the kids, I don't mind the audience."

"I didn't want to bother you."

Kevin knew he was starting to blush as the conversation wore on, turning his pale skin red. He hated it. He knew a blushing redhead was not necessarily his best look.

"You wouldn't be a bother, unless you stood in the way or something." Shin chuckled. "Of course, then, I might just flip over you."

An image of Shin flipping over him formed in Kevin's mind. That was quickly replaced by Shin doing the flip again, completely naked.

Kevin quickly forced it out of his mind, fearing he would turn even redder.

"You okay?" Shin asked, a bigger smile playing across his face, like he knew exactly what Kevin was thinking.

"Yeah. Sorry. It's just... well, you caught me off guard coming over here."

"I didn't think you were ever going to come over there, so I figured I'd make the first move. I can go if you want."

Shin readjusted the pack on his shoulder, as if he were about to leave.

"No. No, that's okay."

"So, why don't you come with me? You can get a front row seat."

"Cool." Kevin worried that he sounded overly excited again, but Shin didn't seem to mind.

Kevin pushed himself off the rock and dropped the chem book and water bottle in his pack. Realizing his shirt was open he hastily began to button it up, suddenly feeling modest.

"You don't have to do that," Shin said. "It's a good look for you."

Kevin stopped halfway and looked at Shin. What did that mean? Was Shin into him? Had they been staring at each other the whole time?

As if to answer the silent question, Shin simply nodded his head.

Kevin unbuttoned the buttons he'd done up and grabbed his pack.

"How long have you been doing parkour?" Kevin asked as they walked.

"Nice. You know what it's called. Sometimes people see it on TV and decide it's cool but don't actually know anything about it."

"Yeah, I've seen it on TV and got hooked. I don't know any of the rules or what the moves are called, but I know it looks really cool."

Shin smiled his biggest smile yet and it nearly melted Kevin from the inside out.

"I've been doing it for about six months now. A friend got me into it, and got me going to a parkour gym. I'm there nearly every morning before school, but I also like coming out here to practice."

"So there's actually a parkour gym in the city?"

"There're a few actually, and some people teach outdoors, too. My friend wants to put a crew together, but we need to get better first."

"That's ambitious," Kevin said as they neared the practice rocks.

Then, without warning, Shin dropped his pack, took off and did a flashy flip over the two closest rocks, turned back and smiled.

Kevin dropped to the grass and sat cross-legged as Shin leaped back onto the rocks he'd just flipped over.

"I bet you could learn this stuff. You look pretty fit."

"I run track. But there's a big difference between that and the stuff you're doing here." Kevin gestured to the rocks.

"It's all teachable. I certainly didn't know what I was doing when I started. I fell on my ass so many times I lost count. I know you've seen me fall while you were perched on that rock of yours."

Kevin didn't know what to say. Why was Shin taking such an interest in him?

"Would you teach me?" The words tumbled out of Kevin's mouth. He'd thought it, but hadn't meant to say it.

"Sure. It'd be cool. You'll probably do better than the kids. I always worry about them getting hurt." Shin offered a hand, helping Kevin up. "I suspect you don't break as easily as a ten year old."

"Probably not," Kevin said brushing grass off his slacks. "I'm tall, but not fragile."

Letting go of his hand, Shin pulled the hem of Kevin's still unbuttoned shirt to the side and gave him a quick once over.

"Definitely lanky," Shin said matter of factly. "But it looks like you've got a good foundation. I mean if you run track, you must have some strength and endurance."

Kevin playfully swatted Shin's hand away and felt himself blush again. Javier was the only other person that had checked him out like that. He was uncomfortable, and excited at the same time.

Shin looked into Kevin's blue-green eyes and raised his eyebrows as if to ask what the problem was.

"Sorry," Kevin said, quietly. "I'm just not..."

"It's okay. But remember, you've looked at me without a shirt on for days." Shin smiled again, and Kevin was glad to see it. "Seems only fair that I get a better look at you. It's hard to do that when you've got the shirt covering you up."

Kevin started to feel emboldened. Was the attraction mutual?

"So you've got a thing for thin, pale white boys?"

Shin put his hand to his chin and considered for a few moments.

"Well, I've got a thing for boys for sure. Pale white boys catch my eye from time to time. One as rail thin as you? Not that I can recall. And none of them have been redheads. But there's always a first time, and on you the whole package looks very, very good."

Damn. He was gay. Freakin' awesome!

They stood there for a while, just looking at each other. They both knew a connection was made. Finally Shin broke the silence.

"So, you wanna give this a try?" Shin asked. "Let's see how you move. Then maybe we go grab a bite to eat."

"Sounds great," Kevin said, trying to keep his excitement from bubbling over too much. "What do you want me to do?"

"Something basic. Just jump from rock to rock like you've seen me doing, but without the flips." Shin jumped suddenly, landing briefly on a nearby rock. "Just move between them," he said.

He jumped again, moving from stone to stone in different ways— sometimes landing on two feet or sometimes one before moving to the next. It looked easy enough.

"Okay," Kevin said. "Here goes."

Kevin stepped back a few paces from the rock he decided would be his start point. Since he worked with hurdles in track he went for a running start and leapt up onto the stone. He tried to weave a different pattern from Shin, sometimes leaping from stone to stone when he thought he could or bouncing on the ground between stones when the distance seemed too great. He teetered a couple times on the uneven rocks, but he never fell. He wanted to finish with some kind of flourish, but didn't as he feared it might end badly.

"See, you did fine. Now it's a matter of adding tricks and flips."

"You mean falling on my head."

"That's part of being a newbie. See this?" Shin asked, stepping close to Kevin and pointing to a scar below his right eye. "One of my first times running out here I fell and banged my head against that rock." He pointed to one of the larger boulders. "That got me a few stitches. But, it didn't mean I wasn't back out here the next day."

Kevin looked at the scar and fought the urge to run his fingers over it.

"Okay. I'm in. Let's see if you can teach me what you do."

"Deal. We start tomorrow. Now let's get some food because I'm starving."

"Sounds good. Lead the way."

They shouldered their backpacks and headed off towards the park's 72nd Street exit. Kevin loved walking with Shin, it already felt like they were more than just friends.

FOUR

THEY DROPPED into a booth at Wok City. This was one of Kevin's favorite places to grab a quick bite. The food was good, cheap and quick, plus it was close to home. Kevin soon learned Shin was a regular as well. Kevin ordered a Chinese chicken salad while Shin got sesame tofu.

"Tofu? Really?"

"What? You went with rabbit food," Shin countered. "Tofu is solid, cheap protein."

"But it tastes like nothing."

"That means you haven't had it prepared right. I'll give you a taste and we'll see what you think. Ru does a fantastic job with it. If he's here, it's what I always get."

"You know the cook?"

"Yeah, my parents know his parents and so I've been coming here for years."

"Cool. I live two blocks away, so I'm here a lot, too."

"Weird how we've never seen each other," Shin said.

"Or, we just didn't notice."

"Who's that big guy I've seen you with?" Shin shifted the conversation.

"Marshall. My best friend since forever. He lives in my building, too. He's a football player and obviously has the body to go with it. He could crush me easily if he wanted. Not that he would on purpose, but if he ever lost his balance and landed on me, it wouldn't end well."

Shin laughed. Kevin did, too. The laughter came easily.

"Nice."

"So you live around here or just like hanging out in the park?" Kevin asked.

"I'm a little further uptown, 110 and Riverside. But I'm down here a lot because I like that part of the park and the rock formations there are some of the best in the city for practice. I also love that it's near the fountain. There's a peacefulness there I really like. I usually stop there every morning to soak it in."

"I like it there, too. I can sit by the fountain for hours," Kevin said.

"I'm embarrassed to say I didn't even know it was there until last year. We learned about it in art class."

"You take art? That's cool. So do I."

"It breaks up the monotony of math. I'm on a stereotypical Asian path, eventually going into theoretical mathematics or something like that."

"That's some pretty intense stuff, but you've still got time to bounce off rocks and study art?"

Shin looked away for a moment. Kevin was afraid he'd said something very wrong.

"The thing is," Shin said, turning back to Kevin, but keeping his voice low, "the school stuff is pretty easy for me. It always has been. I don't know why. My parents both hated school because they had to work hard for their grades. They've done well. My dad works in IT at Google and mom's a history professor at Columbia. Even in kindergarten, I just absorbed knowledge like a sponge. The math is easy and

I enjoy doing it, but I balance it with other stuff that is completely different and a little more challenging."

"That's great," Kevin said, impressed, not put off by what some may have called bragging. "But why did you turn away? Like you were ashamed."

"You can imagine how the geeky, gay kid sometimes gets picked on. That's why I made sure I was strong and fit from middle school on. I wanted to make sure I could defend myself."

Kevin nodded.

"You're more the traditional jock doing track, so I'm guessing you had a better time of it," Shin said as the food arrived.

"I'm an odd jock though. The tall, thin thing gets me picked on depending on who's around. I'm a bookworm, too. I've loved reading since I was little, when mom used to read me *Charlotte's Web* in the tub. I also sketch a lot, so that's usually good for some snarky remarks. Of course, there's the gay thing, but not much gets said about that at my school."

With all the talk, Kevin had forgotten how hungry he was. He quickly started in on his salad while Shin attacked his tofu.

"Here," Shin said suddenly. He offered up his fork, which had a cube of tofu stuck on the end, coated with sesame seeds along with some onion and carrot. A sauce covered all of it. "Try this."

Kevin quickly swallowed his salad and washed it down with some water to clear his palate for the new flavor.

As Kevin leaned in, Shin moved the fork towards his open mouth. Kevin closed his mouth over the food, slipped it off the fork so it could drop onto his tongue. He was immediately hit with the spiciness—not too overpowering, but it certainly had some zip. He didn't taste the blandness or sliminess he generally associated with tofu. The cube was firm and had good texture as he chewed. The flavors were unique. He distinctly tasted the onion and carrot, but he couldn't identify what was in the sauce that made it so delicious.

"Damn, that's tasty."

Kevin licked his lips trying to eek out as much of that flavor as possible. It made his salad seem boring, even though it had a zesty dressing of its own.

"Told you. As long as you see Ru in the kitchen, you can order this. It's okay when the other cooks do it, but it's really his dish. He's at the grill now." Shin pointed towards the kitchen.

Kevin turned and saw a young man busily working several orders.

"I see him here a lot."

"Yeah, he co-owns the place with his parents now. He bought a share of the restaurant from them a couple years ago. Most days he's cooking, but he does take a day off every week so sometimes you get a different cook."

The boys munched in silence for a while. Kevin found it to be a comfortable silence, like he'd known Shin for years instead of only an hour.

"So I've told you my thing for math. What's your college thing going to be?"

"Architecture. I've been interested by buildings and how they're put together forever. It started with blocks when I was like five and later it was Legos, Tinkertoys, Erector Sets, Lincoln Logs, whatever. Sometimes I'd use them all in the same structure."

"You still build?"

"Oh yeah," Kevin said, proud that he hadn't outgrown building things. "I still buy new stuff sometimes, too. Sometimes Lego releases new blocks that I must have, or I'll buy replacement parts if I decide to keep something built. I don't do that too often since I don't have a lot of space, but I like to keep some of my favorite builds around for a while."

"I'd love to see them sometime."

Kevin pulled his phone from his pocket and flicked over to the photo gallery. He had a folder full of things he'd built.

"I take pictures of everything. That way I have a record even if I don't keep it built for very long."

He handed the phone over to Shin who swiped through the pictures.

"These are so cool," he said after looking at a few of them. "So many different types of things. I like how you take so many pictures of each, both close-up and wide shots, and the angles are pretty dramatic, too."

Kevin smiled. "Thanks. You've got a good eye. Plus, I want to document everything in case I want to recreate it later."

"How many of these have you built?"

"It must be in the hundreds. I've got pictures that go back three or four years. I figured out in seventh grade that architecture was what I wanted to do so I've kept photos or drawings ever since."

"Seventh grade, really?"

"Yeah. Career day. One of the moms was an architect. I heard her presentation and saw the models she brought. I talked to her afterwards. Probably asked some really stupid questions, but she let me come watch her work a few days that summer and I was hooked. We've stayed in touch and I'm hoping I can intern, or something, at her firm this summer. Be good to soak up some knowledge and it'll look good on college apps."

"Maybe I can see them in person some time." Shin said, handing back the phone.

"That can be arranged," Kevin said with a smile as he finished up his salad. "So why theoretical mathematics? What do you do with that?"

"It can be the foundation for a lot of things, like economics. There are a lot of paths in grad school, too. I haven't quite decided what I'm going to do with it long term. I lean towards teaching so I can try and get other students as excited about it as I am."

"Good to have options."

"Exactly," Shin said, as he mopped up the sauce with a last bit of tofu.

"So what's goin' on for the rest of your afternoon?" Kevin asked, hoping they were not about to go their separate ways.

"I've got a paper on the Civil War to work on and some reading for art history. But I've also met this guy and he could be a welcome distraction."

Kevin grinned.

"What about you?" Shin asked.

"I've got some chem reading to finish. You have your books with you?"

"Yeah."

"Why don't you come to my place? I can show you some of my buildings, we can keep talking, maybe get some studying done."

"Perfect."

FIVE

As THE GUYS arrived at Kevin's building, Marshall was coming out. He took a look at the duo and grinned as he came down the building's stairs onto the sidewalk.

"Shin, this is my best friend, Marshall. Marshall, this is Shin, the guy I've been watching in the park. He introduced himself today."

"Nice to meet the guy that's caught Kevin's eye."

Marshall and Shin nodded at each other.

"Good to meet you, Marshall. I think I saw you there a couple times, right?"

"Yeah. I was a witness to the stalking."

"It's a good friend that endures that."

"He's done it for me a couple times, so it's all good. I gotta get goin' guys. Mom's got me running errands before she gets home. I'll catch you later. Good to meet you, Shin."

"You too Marshall. Hope to see you again."

Shin went up the stairs first, which gave Kevin a quick moment to mouth "oh my god" to Marshall as he passed. Marshall nodded and smiled, knowing he'd get all the details later.

Once inside, they took the stairs and reached the fourth floor in no time. After entering 4R, Kevin led them through the living room into a small hallway on the opposite side. Kevin's room was at the very end.

The room was tiny. Outside of a single bed, desk, with a window above it, and a dresser, there wasn't a lot of room for much else. But somehow Kevin had managed to fit in a work table and a small wardrobe since the room had no closet. Loaded book shelves and a few posters occupied most of the walls. It was a lot of things in a small space, but it didn't feel cramped or crowded. It felt clean, organized, as if everything was where it should be.

"This fits you. Lived in, comfortable but ordered, too."

"Thanks," Kevin said, smiling appreciatively.

Shin's attention wandered over to the Lego and Erector Set skyscraper growing out of the top of the dresser and he went to it immediately.

"This is incredible. I've never seen anything like it," Shin said running his hand gingerly over the Legos and the skin of steel pieces.

"It was a different sort of thing to make. A building that sort of twists, like a piece of corkscrew pasta. The Legos are the bricks the building would be built out of and the steel is a contrasting material for visual interest. I have no idea if this building would be practical, but it looks cool."

"Maybe you'll discover how to make it work."

"It would be exciting to build something completely new and unique." Kevin picked up a house from the nearby bookshelf. "This is one of my favorites. It's my dream house, at least until I come up with something better. It's sort of my own take on a Frank Lloyd Wright."

Shin studied the model as Kevin held it, getting close to it and then stepping away to take it in from a far. He reached out, but then pulled back before he touched it.

"It's okay. You can touch it. Hold it. Move it. Whatever. It's built strong."

"Cool."

Shin took it and held it, turning it so he could see the sides and back.

"Nice, you even built a deck with possibly the tiniest set of sliding doors I've ever seen."

"It's all about the details. I envision this house backing up to a wooded lot. Sort of my own Central Park behind the house."

Kevin pointed to another building on the shelf.

"This is another favorite, though it's more fragile," Kevin said. "I went for a dome-inspired structure with this one."

This model was made from Legos along with Tinkertoy accents. There were several domes linked together with some round Tinkertoy pieces inserted into the domed roofs with wooden pegs running around the base, acting as a border to the structure. Several patches of each dome included clear blocks, some painted to resemble solar panels.

"Not only do I like the design, I love that you're able to do this stuff with Legos. Both this one and the skyscraper are killer. Where'd you learn how to do this?"

"Trial and error," Kevin said, with pride. "Even after building for years, sometimes I still can't build the things I see in my head. I can't wait to get to college and learn how to make stuff that's really cool and structurally sound."

Shin put the house back in its place and headed to the work table for a look at the project Kevin was currently working on. There were sketches of a long, flat structure and the beginnings of it built mostly out of Tinkertoy sticks.

"This one's a lark." Kevin said. "Plans for a base on another planet."

"I didn't take you for a sci-fi geek. I like that trait in a guy very much."

Shin looked over the detailed drawings, which showed an overhead view as well as a couple profile views.

"Your drawing is amazing," Shin said. "There's so much detail."

"Thanks. I tend to draw everything I build. And there are far more drawings than there are models. Some of the stuff I draw, I can't figure out how to build. Plus the drawings take up a lot less space than the models. I've got tons of sketch books because I refuse to throw them out."

"You're an impressive guy, Kevin."

Involuntarily, Kevin turned away and made busy work of tidying up the stray building blocks. He didn't know how to respond to the compliment, other than to turn red.

Shin stepped in behind him, close enough that parts of them were touching. Shin's stomach against Kevin's lower back. Shin's quad against the back of his leg. Kevin shifted the drawings on the work top as Shin's hand covered one of his.

"Sorry. I didn't mean to embarrass you."

Kevin turned to face Shin and found him just inches away. They regarded each other close up. The thick hair on Shin's head, styled so that it stood up in the front and flattened out towards the back, was something Kevin wanted to run his hands through. He wanted to see it without product too, in its natural state. Full lips called to Kevin for a kiss, but he thought that might be moving too fast.

"It's okay."

"You're cute when you're flustered," Shin said in a whisper.

No one moved as they continued to stare. Kevin's insides fluttered, reminding him what it was like to be this close to someone he was attracted to.

Kevin gave in and inched closer to Shin, who kept his body still. As Shin began to smile, Kevin went for it. Their lips touched ever so gently as Kevin puckered and planted a small kiss that Shin returned just as delicately.

As they continued to kiss, Kevin reached up to do what he'd wanted to do—run his hand through Shin's hair. It felt great as he gently pulled Shin's head closer so the kisses wouldn't stop. Shin moaned quietly. Kevin didn't know if it was the kissing or playing with his hair, so he kept doing both.

Shin faintly tasted of the sauce from the tofu. It tasted good on him. Shin's smell was good too, just a bit musky owing to his workout in the park.

Shin moved his whole body into Kevin's so that they were fully touching each other. Kevin, since he was around six inches taller, angled his head down to keep the all important contact with Shin's delicious mouth.

There kisses went from fevered to gentle, as hands wandered slowly over clothing, sometimes checking out what was beneath. Kevin liked Shin's hard, packed muscles, a sharp contrast to his own. He hoped Shin didn't mind the difference.

Suddenly Shin stopped.

"Can I do something? Something I've wanted to do for a couple hours now?"

Kevin couldn't imagine what this was.

"Um...sure."

Silently Shin reached out and unbuttoned Kevin's shirt. He went slow, revealing the patches of milky white skin peppered with the occasional freckle. When he was done, he pushed the white shirt off Kevin's shoulders, revealing even more freckles. Kevin shrugged it off his arms and let it fall to the floor. He stood still while Shin looked at him.

"You may be lanky, but you look great."

The blush washed over Kevin again. He didn't let himself turn away this time.

"Thank you," he said as he took a step forward and grabbed a fist full of Shin's t-shirt. "You need to lose this, too."

Kevin reached behind and grabbed the hem of Shin's t-shirt and lifted it up. Shin dutifully raised his arms so Kevin could pull it over his head. Kevin was in awe. The muscle definition in Shin's chest and abs was impressive. His bulging biceps and triceps were stunning.

"I knew you were built. But up close, like this, it's amazing."

Kevin ran his hand slowly over Shin's pecs and down over the defined abs.

"Thanks," Shin said softly.

As Kevin's hands gently moved over Shin's body, Shin laughed a little.

"What? Ticklish?" Kevin asked, stopping, but not removing his hand.

"No. It's not that. You're just so white. I mean I'm not very dark at all, but against your skin it's like I've got a good tan."

"Curse of the redhead, paler than the average white guy."

Kevin pivoted them towards the mirror that hung on the back of the door. They stood side by side.

"We make a striking couple," Kevin said. "Our height, skin, red hair versus black."

"We should go on a date and solidify this couple thing," Shin said as he continued to compare their reflections.

"I'd like that," Kevin said, absently running his hand over Shin's.

There was a loud bang as the apartment's front door opened and closed. The boys froze.

Kevin looked at his watch and grimaced. "When did it get so late?" he said quietly. "I didn't realize it was past five already."

"Are you going to get in trouble?" Shin asked, keeping his voice to a whisper.

"Nah. I've had friends over after school before," Kevin said, picking his shirt up from the floor. "But we should get dressed." He pulled the shirt on and quickly buttoned it up.

"Got it," Shin said, slipping back into his tee. "So what'll we do for this date?"

"I'd be good doing just about anything as long as it's with you."

"Anyone home?" Kevin's mom called from elsewhere in the apartment.

"Yeah, mom. I'm here. Have a friend over, too."

The clicking of her heels announced her approach. Kevin quickly opened the door.

"Hey, mom."

"Hi, Kevin. Good day?" his mom asked standing in the doorway.

"An excellent day. Mom, this is my new friend, Shin."

Shin went to Kevin's mom with his hand extended. "Pleasure to meet you, Mrs. ... Uhm..." He grinned and looked back at Kevin. "I don't actually know your last name."

Kevin laughed. "Sorry, it's McCollum."

"Nice to meet you, Mrs. McCollum."

Kevin's mom laughed, too. "Good to meet you, Shin. Where'd you two meet?"

"I've been watching him run parkour in the park for a couple week's now, but we finally talked to each other today. I was showing him some of my models and stuff."

"That's nice," she said as she looked at her watch. "We do need to get dinner started, Kevin. Shin, you're welcome to stay if you'd like."

"Thanks, Mrs. McCollum, but I should get going. Need to finish up my homework." Shin looked back to Kevin.

"Another time then," Kevin's mom said before she turned and went down the hall to the master bedroom. "See you in the kitchen in a few minutes."

Kevin and Shin headed to the front door.

"Gimme your phone," Kevin said.

Shin unlocked his phone and handed it over. Kevin open the dialer and entered his number. "Now you've got my number, and," he paused as his own phone rang from his pocket, "I've got yours."

"Perfect," Shin said, accepting his phone back. "See you at the rocks tomorrow?"

"Definitely."

SIX

KEVIN WAS BEYOND NERVOUS. Actually he was terrified. It was the night of their first official date. It'd only been a week since they'd first met, and the crazy first kisses were still fresh in his memory. Kevin played them back over and over in his head every night before falling asleep.

They'd spent nearly every afternoon in the park together, missing only one day when Shin had a lab project to work on after school. The other days they talked and talked, and Shin taught Kevin a little parkour, too.

What terrified Kevin most of all was meeting Shin's parents. Shin always spoke highly of them. He said they'd been good to the two other boys he'd brought home. They already knew Shin was seeing someone new, so it wouldn't be a complete surprise to them.

Kevin had also met Javier's parents. That had been scary, too. There was no date that night. Instead he had dinner at Javier's house because his parents wanted to meet the boy Javier hung out with. It was nothing but stressful.

Tonight was a double whammy. The parents wanted to have tea

before the guys headed out to the Idoltones concert. Tea could be easy, or it could be an inquisition.

Kevin arrived promptly at Shin's brownstone. He'd been here a few days earlier to borrow some parkour DVDs, but Shin's parents had been at work so he didn't meet them. Kevin buzzed apartment three and checked his reflection in the glass door to make sure it was just right before anyone checked the camera to let him in.

The screen under the camera flickered to life. Shin's sexy face filled the monitor.

"Kevin!" Shin shouted loud enough that most of the people on the sidewalk must've heard it. "Right on time, of course. Come on up."

Shin's face disappeared and a buzz sounded releasing the door. Kevin took a deep breath, went in, and bounded up the stairs.

Shin was waiting for him at the door and as soon as he was inside gave him a big hug.

"Good to see you," Shin said, walking him towards the living room. "Aren't you a tiny bit over dressed for where we're going?"

Shin wore jeans and a black t-shirt that looked like it'd been splattered with red paint. Kevin, also in jeans, wore a more conservative dark green Polo shirt.

"Dude, I couldn't wear this to meet your parents." Kevin lifted up the Polo revealing a well-worn Idoltones t-shirt and a black studded belt. "Don't worry, I'll look right for the show."

"You didn't have to dress for them. Geez. They know we're going to the concert."

"Come on, you know me well enough that I'm going to dress up to meet your parents."

"Just sayin', I met your mom in a sweaty t-shirt and shorts." Shin saw the look on Kevin's face and knew he'd never win. He smiled, letting it go. "Right, right. It's all part of what I've come to love about you," Shin said as they entered the living room.

The room was comfortable, striking the right balance between formal and casual. Kevin found it tastefully decorated, the furnishings and artwork minimalist in nature. Shin's parents were on a simple tan couch, facing away from the door. They stopped talking and stood as the boys entered.

"Mom, dad, this is Kevin."

Their smiles faltered as they caught their first look at the couple. Kevin's stomach immediately did a somersault. Something was definitely wrong. He worried he might have something to do with it.

"Kevin, this is my mom and dad." Shin seemed oblivious to his parents' reaction.

Kevin's good manners kicked in and he went for it.

"Mr. and Mrs. Tanaka, it's great to meet you both."

He extended a hand to Shin's dad. It was a quick, brusk two shakes and Mr. Tanaka released it. It felt like a brush off, but Kevin wasn't sure. Maybe that was just how Shin's dad shook hands. He extended his hand to Mrs. Tanaka who gave a brief, dainty shake.

"Nice to meet you Kevin," she said, sounding strained.

"I need to make a call," Mr. Tanaka said suddenly. "You'll excuse me, please."

"Of course," Kevin said. He was really starting to freak out and was doing everything he could to stay calm.

"Dad?" Shin called out as his dad left the room. There was disappointment in his voice. He was clued in that something was amiss.

A few moments later a door opened and closed elsewhere in the apartment.

"My apologies," Mrs. Tanaka said, still strained, but not missing a beat. She had a slight accent, very similar to Mr. Tanaka's. "Things periodically come up that he has to attend to."

It seemed as if she was trying to establish some normalcy in the unexpected absence of her husband. Kevin glanced over at Shin. He looked completely devastated.

He wanted to give him a hug to make him feel better, but that didn't seem appropriate given the vibe in the room. Asking what was wrong also seemed inappropriate. He didn't want to make Shin any more uncomfortable than he already was. So Kevin did the only thing he could, be a good guest.

"I love this room, Mrs. Tanaka. It's absolutely beautiful. That Gris is one of my favorite works. I saw some of his work at the Met last year." Kevin went to the painting, which was hanging over the fireplace.

"Thank you, Kevin. How would you like your tea? It's Oolong."

"Nothing in it please. I like Oolong just as it is."

"You know tea?"

"I know the Oolong," Kevin said, taking the seat Mrs. Tanaka indicated on the couch. "My parents, on the other hand, know tea and have a lot of it in the house. I prefer Oolong because it seems to have some backbone."

"Indeed."

She smiled and Kevin thought he might have made some progress. He stole a look at Shin who was preparing his tea, his head down. He'd never seen Shin look so distressed and didn't know what he could do to fix it. They'd be on their way soon and hopefully they'd talk about whatever was happening.

For the next twenty minutes the conversation continued, if somewhat hesitantly. Shin was quiet, but Kevin and Mrs. Tanaka talked. Kevin learned out about her work at Columbia. She asked about his school. She seemed interested in what Kevin wanted to pursue and he even showed some pictures of his models. They talked about art, too, going back to the Gris and even discussing cubism for a few minutes.

Shin spoke up when it was time to go and then it was only to get them out of the room. He hardly addressed his mother at all. As they headed to Shin's room so Kevin could lose his Polo, Shin's father called out for Shin to come see him. Shin winced when he heard his name.

"Back in a minute," he said, sounding like he'd been summoned to the principal's office. "Make yourself at home."

Shin left him. Kevin waited in his room, feeling not very

welcome. While his chat with Mrs. Tanaka had been pleasant enough, he felt like she was only being polite, and that she did not genuinely like him.

He stripped off his shirt, folded it and placed it on the trunk at the foot of Shin's bed. He sat quietly in the desk chair, waiting for him to come back. Shin was only gone a few minutes, but it felt like an eternity. He'd heard no yelling, but Shin looked as if he'd been beaten down.

"Ready to go?" Shin asked, trying, but failing, to sound like nothing was wrong.

"Um. Sure."

Kevin wasn't going to push for details until they were out of the apartment.

"Cool." Shin headed for the door and Kevin followed. Shin's body language was totally different, and Kevin had never seen him like this before. His walk was stilted, and his body seemed stiff and rigid, almost as if it was painful to move.

Once they were on the street, Shin walked so fast that Kevin had to hustle to keep up. It seemed Shin wanted to put some distance between himself and home as quickly as possible. When they stopped at a crosswalk, Kevin put a hand on Shin's shoulder in an effort to force him to slow down when the light turned.

"Slow up, man. What's going on? What did I do?"

They looked at each other for the first time since leaving the apartment. Shin's furrowed brow and lack of smile made his distress clear.

"You didn't do anything. I promise. That was my fault."

They started walking again, and Shin moved at a slower pace.

"How is it your fault? You didn't do anything except introduce me. Your parents looked upset the moment they saw me. Did I wear the wrong thing? Should I have done something different? We can go back and I'll apologize."

Shin looked briefly at Kevin as they navigated traffic on the busy sidewalk.

"There was nothing you could've done different. It's really my fault." Shin sighed. "I didn't bring home a Japanese boy."

Kevin stopped walking. Everything had been so perfect the past week and now this. The most exciting guy he'd met since Javier moved, or maybe ever, and now he might lose him because his parents didn't approve.

Shin turned back when he realized Kevin wasn't following.

"Look, I told dad I wasn't going to stop seeing you. It's a ridiculous old custom. I didn't even know they expected it. Yes, the only other guys I brought home were Japanese. Actually, that's not true, one was Korean but we didn't date long enough for them to find out. And you definitely can't pass as Japanese."

Kevin laughed, a little louder than he planned, considering the circumstances. But Shin was right. No one was going to think he was anything other than white.

When Shin didn't join in, he regretted the brief chuckle.

"It's me that owes you an apology," Shin continued. "I wouldn't have put you in that situation if I'd known they would react that way. It wasn't fair to you. I'd even told them your name, but I guess *Kevin* didn't necessarily mean you weren't Japanese. My parents, especially my dad, treated you very badly."

"Your mom tried to recover though. We had a good talk."

"Please don't try to make her behavior okay. It's not how I was raised to treat a guest and I'm furious they treated you like that." Shin stopped them just before the steps down to the subway. "I'm falling for you pretty hard and I don't want their old fashioned crap getting in the way of that. They accept that I'm gay. They need to accept that I'm in love with a very handsome and awesome white guy." Shin let that hang in the air for a moment before speaking again. "Now, come on, we're going to be late if we don't get moving and I don't want to be stuck at the back of the crowd."

Kevin followed down the stairs and they hurried through the gates to catch the train that was pulling into the station. Kevin's head was spinning, trying to process everything Shin had said. It had gone from "I'm falling for you pretty hard" to "I'm in love with" in just a few words. Kevin felt sad and elated at the same time. Worst case, Kevin had never imagined tea would go as badly as it did. He just expected it to be awkward or uncomfortable. On the other hand, Shin said he loved him.

"You should know," Kevin said, as they settled on the train, "that I'm falling in love with you, too. Getting to know you over the past week's been awesome."

Shin took Kevin's hand in his as they rode the train.

"Look, I'm going to talk to them. They need to understand how I feel about you. But, I don't want this to spoil our date. We've been looking forward to this, so let's have a great time."

"Okay," Kevin said. "We'll have a rockin' good time at the show and we'll deal with this tomorrow."

"Now, no more talk about parents."

They got out of the subway just a couple blocks from Irving Plaza and got in early enough that they were near the stage for the show.

SEVEN

"THANKS FOR A GREAT NIGHT," Kevin said as he hugged Shin on the stairs outside his building. Shin stood one step up from Kevin so they'd be face to face. It was almost one in the morning, and while the street was still bustling, the boys acted as if they were alone.

"I should be the one thanking you," Shin said after nibbling on Kevin's lower lip. "The show was amazing. I think I've got a new favorite band." Shin pulled them even closer together. "I'll see you tomorrow, right?"

"Yup. At two by the rocks."

They kissed again before Shin slowly stepped backwards down to the sidewalk, never losing eye contact with Kevin. As he turned to go, he almost ran into Marshall, who was just coming home. "Oh, hey, Marshall."

"Hey, guys," Marshall said. "How was the show?"

"Amazing," Kevin said, as he bounced down from the steps to join them. "Idoltones were in spectacular form."

"I loved it," Shin said. "I'm going to grab some downloads as soon as I get home."

"Cool," Marshall said.

"What'd you get up to tonight?" Shin asked.

"Went to a photography exhibit with Cassie. Not my usual sort of thing, but she made it okay." Marshall had a grin on his face that Kevin appreciated seeing, especially since his night had been rough.

"Nothing wrong with that," Shin said. "I gotta get goin' guys. Marshall, you should come by the rocks tomorrow and watch me put him through his paces."

"Sounds good," Marshall said. "See ya, Shin."

"Bye," Kevin said as he leaned in for a final kiss. Kevin felt Marshall watching him as he watched Shin go.

"So the show was good. How was the date?" Marshall asked after Shin turned a corner and was out of sight.

"Good and horrible at the same time." Kevin turned to face Marshall. "Meeting his parents was an epic disaster."

"Uh-oh. I thought he was out."

"He's out. Has been for almost four years. I'm not the first guy he's brought home. What they weren't expecting was a white boy."

"Oh shit," Marshall said as they sat down on the stairs. "How did he not know that?"

"I guess they've never talked about it. The other guys were Asian. The whole thing was horrible. Shin met me at the door all excited, but when his parents saw me, his father made up some excuse and left, leaving me, Shin and his mom alone. We talked but it was really awkward, and Shin barely said a word. Then, before we left, Shin spoke with his dad who told him I was unacceptable." Kevin looked away. "And we hardly talked about it afterwards."

"Damn," said Marshall, shaking his head. "I had no idea that sort of thing still happened. What's he going to do?"

"I've no idea. I don't think he does either. We're gonna hang out tomorrow, maybe he'll have talked to his dad some more by then." Kevin looked over at his friend. "What chance do I have with him? If the competition was with another guy, fine. But his parents?"

"Don't be so fatalistic. Give Shin a chance to work it out. There's no reason to think it's over. He came out as gay, so maybe he'll be able to come out as loving a white boy, too."

"I hope you're right. His mom seemed like she'd be cool. Maybe he can bring her over to our side."

"Let's get upstairs. We'll make some popcorn and watch a crappy movie."

"Before the movie, I need more details on your date. You saying the exhibit was good means that Cassie worked some kinda magic on you."

Marshall stood up and offered Kevin a hand. "Yeah, she was awesome."

Kevin pulled himself up and smiled, happy for the distraction, otherwise he'd be replaying the tea scene over and over in his head as he tried to go to sleep.

EIGHT

Gyms intimidated Kevin. He always felt self-conscious because of his lankiness. Even though he'd been working out with Shin, he still felt out of place among the weights and the weight-lifters.

Being with Shin made it easier though. And this gym had the proper equipment for parkour training, including a massive rock wall. Shin seemed to know a lot of the people here, and had introduced him as his boyfriend, which Kevin liked a lot. It meant Shin didn't feel ashamed of him, or that he felt like the relationship needed to be hidden.

Shin's friends seemed pretty cool with him dating Kevin. They made him feel welcome. There were four of them using the parkour equipment and they gladly folded Kevin into their rotation.

It was brutal. Shin was killing Kevin slowly, making him do circuits of going up the rock wall as fast as he could coupled with a series of box jumps when he got to the floor. Kevin understood the need for both, and he liked the box jumps. His legs were already strong from track. His arm strength on the rock wall was another matter and he hated it after the second climb.

Kevin was scaling the wall a fourth time when he heard a new voice below. None of Shin's friends seemed to respond to the newcomer with enthusiasm, their voices growing louder as they talked. Shin minded his safety rope and Kevin could tell Shin was still keeping watch over him, despite the commotion. Everyone below was speaking what he assumed to be Japanese.

Shin had never spoken Japanese around him. He wasn't even sure Shin spoke it at all. He had no accent when speaking English, and his parents barely had one. Perhaps it was because they'd lived here for decades, and Shin was born and raised in the city. Regardless, Kevin hoped Shin spoke the language so that maybe he'd learn a little Japanese, too.

Kevin touched the top of the wall.

"Alright, coming down," he called to Shin.

"Okay. Come down diagonally instead of straight. Think about how to place your feet and hands to zig zag. It's a good agility exercise. I'll keep the rope out of the way."

Kevin took a deep breath. This wasn't going to be easy. "Okay." He tried to sound confident.

He looked down for the next place to put his feet. Going down the same way he'd come up was hard enough. It wasn't like he was on a ladder with easy-to-find steps. Going down and sideways would be trickier. But he was determined not to let himself come free of the wall. Even though he was a newbie, he didn't want to disappoint Shin, or himself.

"You can do this, Kevin," Shin called up. "Just go slow."

Shin's words emboldened him. He climbed down two rungs, steps... he wasn't quite sure what to call it. He went slowly, his movements measured. Down below the newcomer was getting louder and louder. Shin's friends matched his volume, the conversation getting more heated. Then the newcomer's tone changed. Kevin didn't need to understand Japanese to know sarcasm when he heard it.

"*Omae, juubun yaro?*" Shin suddenly called out, clearly angry.

Kevin paused his descent. He'd never heard that tone from Shin and it surprised him. It was clear Shin was pissed, and that he spoke Japanese.

"D take the rope. Kevin, keep doing what you're doing. D won't let anything happen."

Kevin felt the rope tension change for a moment as it passed from Shin to D. Kevin liked D, which was what Daisuke preferred to be called, and trusted him. D was Shin's best friend. It'd be like Kevin leaving Shin in Marshall's care.

Kevin looked down, waiting for a sign from D that he was ready. Before he refocused on the descent, Kevin watched Shin grab the stranger by the shoulders, spin him around and push him towards the exit. It was aggressive and, again, unlike anything Kevin had seen before.

D tugged on the rope. "Go ahead," he said.

Kevin resumed his descent, but picked up the pace as he was eager to get down and find out what was going on. D did a solid job with the rope and even provided coaching if Kevin was about to make a misstep. Kevin only goofed up a hand position once, but he had a firm enough grip with the other that he didn't need the spot.

It took only two minutes for Kevin to get down, but it felt like forever. He was glad to have his feet finally touch the ground.

"What's up between Shin and that other guy?" Kevin asked D as he unclipped from the rope so he could do the box jumps.

D looked at Kevin and then at the other guys who were around them, but no one stepped up with details.

"You really should ask Shin," D said, as he put the spotting rope away. "I'm not sure it's my place."

"Fine," Kevin said, mildly annoyed. "Where'd they go?"

Kevin looked around and when he saw them, he headed in their direction. D grabbed his arm.

"Let them finish."

"Why?"

D looked uncomfortable.

"Okay, it's not like Quan was trying to keep it quiet, you just didn't understand." D spoke softly, not wanting to spread everything around the gym a second time. "Quan is Shin's ex. The first one."

Kevin nodded. He'd heard the name before. Shin and Quan's breakup had been a nasty one, thanks in part to Quan's very negative attitude. Shin joked that Quan would be right at home on *Real Housewives of New York* and wasn't the right kind of guy for him.

"Quan told Shin that he wouldn't be having trouble with his parents if they were still together."

Kevin felt like he'd been kicked in the stomach.

"How does he know about that?"

"Their families go way back. Their parents are good friends, their grandparents, too. Shin's never been able to keep much from Quan because of that. Maybe Quan's parents told him, or maybe he eavesdropped. I wouldn't put it past him."

Kevin was speechless. D put his arm around Kevin's shoulders.

"Look, I'm not sure I should say this, but I've already said a lot, so here goes. Shin really likes you. You're the first guy he's gone out with that I like. I see how well you two click. He talks about you constantly. This thing with his parents is hard for him because he's so close to them. This is really the first issue they've ever had. He's trying to figure out a way to make them see that dating you is okay. Quan shouldn't be interfering. If Shin hadn't called him on it, I was going to. It's not his business."

"Can I ask you something?"

The guys nearby pretended not to listen to them, focusing instead on their workout.

"Sure." D looked more at ease now.

"What's your take on this?"

"I think Shin has a good thing with you. He's definitely happy, even with his parent's on his case. I think you're a good guy. As his best friend I'm happy he's happy. I don't like what his parents are putting him through though. I mean I get it, but I don't. This is the twenty-first century and I don't know why this tradition hangs on for some. I'm lucky my parents aren't making me do it. Toshi," D gestured behind him at one of the guys Kevin met earlier, "is expected to date Japanese girls. He's secretly seeing someone from El Salvador. So, you see, Shin's not the only one with these problems."

"Thanks. I guess that's good to know."

D nodded. "Is Shin talking to you about all this?"

"I ask him how things are at home every couple days. He doesn't want to talk about it and I don't know how much I should push."

"He needs to talk to you. It's not fair for him to leave you out." Shin came back towards the group. "You should get to the box jumps," D said, changing the conversation before Shin was within earshot. Kevin was glad for D's quick thinking. He'd admit to Shin he'd talked with D later. "Hop up, hop down then hop up on the next one and keep moving between the various sizes. Try not to over think the jumps, just keep moving."

"Got it."

D nodded again and started putting away some of the other equipment they'd used. Kevin was jumping as Shin arrived. He tried to look upbeat, but Kevin could see that Quan had gotten under his skin.

"Sorry about that," Shin said. "That was Quan and sometimes Quan doesn't know when to shut up. How'd your descent go?"

"Not bad," Kevin said, as he jumped. "D guided me well and I made it with only one real stumble. He never had to catch me, though."

"Good."

Shin watched as Kevin performed a series of random box jumps. The boxes were like the rocks they used in the park, except easier to land on because of their smooth surface. Kevin tried to vary his jumps as much as possible, sometimes going from box to box, or jumping down to the floor and back up again.

"You're getting better at this. Your movements are more fluid, which is great. We need to focus more on your grip strength and upper body."

"You should make him go vertical more often," D said, coming back from the storage locker. "He's doing good on the wall."

"Sound good?" Shin asked Kevin as he stopped in front of them.

"Sounds hard, but I'm game."

Shin smiled. "Excellent. I'll have you doing flips on your own in no time."

"I don't know about that."

"Oh come on, it's easy," Shin said as he did a front flip standing right in front of Kevin.

"He's right. Super easy." D started doing the same thing.

"Show offs," Kevin said, walking away from them to get his towel to wipe the sweat off his face.

"I don't know what he's talking about," said Shin as they continued flipping.

"Me either."

Goofing off was lightening Shin's mood, and that was good. At least he wasn't dwelling on Quan. But, D was right, Shin needed to keep him in the loop about what was going on so it wouldn't blow up in their faces.

"Okay, I'm going to grab a shower while you guys keep doing whatever this is."

As Kevin walked into the locker room, they continued flipping as their friends egged them on.

Kevin quickly found his locker, stripped out of his sweaty clothes and slipped a towel around his waist.

"You should know, he'll never be able to stay with you," said a heavily accented voice directly behind Kevin.

Kevin turned. Quan stood there, arms folded across his chest. Kevin frowned. There was no reason to hide his dislike for the guy who was giving Shin grief.

"He may defy his parents for a while," Quan continued, "but ultimately he'll decide to honor tradition and pick a guy who'll make him and his parents happy."

"Even if that's true, I don't think he'll choose you."

Kevin studied Quan. The guy radiated negativity, everything from his stance to the way he talked. He had a lithe, muscular body and the tight clothes he wore left nothing to the imagination. Without the muscles, he probably would have been as lanky as Kevin. At first glance, Quan and Shin probably had been a cute couple, but after only a few minutes it was clear there was nothing cute about Quan at all. Shin and D's intense dislike of him made total sense.

"Maybe. Doesn't mean I won't be able to try, unlike you who'll lose no matter what."

Kevin stepped forward slowly clenching his fist. He didn't have the muscle Quan did, but he had height and he wasn't going to take any crap from this jerk.

"He's rejected you once," Kevin said, sounding forceful, "so why don't you just leave it alone."

"Or what? Scrawny Red's going to hurt me?" Quan stepped forward closing more of the space between them.

"What the fuck, Quan?" Shin said coming up behind Kevin.

"Someone needs to let Red know how this is going to play out. He shouldn't even be in the running for you."

"That's my call, not yours," Shin said, standing beside Kevin and taking his hand. D came up on Kevin's other side.

"Then you're all delusional," Quan said, his bravado fading now that he was out-numbered.

"Quan, you should go," D said.

"Fine. But you and Shin know I'm right. This boy's just a distraction."

Quan turned down a row of lockers so he didn't have to pass them on his way out.

"What an asshole," Kevin said.

"Guys, let's forget about him and go grab some pizza," D said.

"Sounds good," Shin said. "What about the other guys?"

"They can join us if they hurry up," D said, "otherwise we'll tell them where to find us."

"Don't mess with D when he gets hungry," Shin said, looking to Kevin.

"Let's go then. And I'm definitely in for pizza."

The guys cleaned up quickly. As they dressed, they talked about the parkour competition that was coming to the Meadowlands in a few weeks, and asked Kevin if he'd like to join them.

Kevin was thrilled to be invited. He wanted Marshall to meet D and hang out with the group, so this might be the perfect thing. Shin had already met Marshall and sometimes the three of them hung out after school. D was awesome, so it would be great if they could all get together.

D took the lead as they left the gym, heading to a pizza place a few blocks away. It was just the three of them since the others had stayed behind to finish their workout.

"This is one of the two best pizza places in the city, I think," D said.

"Excellent. What's the other one?" Kevin asked.

"Two Boots in Brooklyn."

"That one I know. We lived in the Slope for a while and Two Boots was awesome. I still go there sometimes when I'm craving a slice of their pepperoni. It's the best."

"Sweet. Someone else who knows good pizza," D said. "That definitely goes into your plus column."

"Dare I ask what's in the negative?"

"Right now, it's empty."

"It takes a lot to get negatives with D," Shin said as they entered the pizza place. "But it can happen. Quan's negative column is over-flowing."

D laughed. "Yeah. He was earning poor marks from the moment I met him. You've done much better picking a boyfriend this time."

The guys went to the counter to order from the half-dozen pies on display.

"What do you recommend?" Kevin asked D.

"If you're a true carnivore, you can't go wrong with the meat lovers," D said, pointing to one of the pizzas that was loaded with every meat possible. "I call it the pig pizza for obvious reasons."

"Be careful with that," Shin said. "It's an insane slice. Don't follow his example, he can scarf down two or three slices like it's nothing."

"It looks good. But, yeah, I'll start with just one of those."

"Get more, we need to bulk you up," D said.

"I don't think I need that kind of bulk," Kevin said.

As expected, D went for two slices of pig pizza. Shin had a sensible slice of the veggie and one with just pepperoni. Kevin picked up a slice of pig along with a margarita, which was his favorite.

"I didn't realize how hungry I was until now," Kevin said as they sat down.

"You just finished ninety minutes of bouncing around and climbing. What did you expect?" Shin asked, his mouth full of food.

Kevin shrugged as he tore into the pig pizza. The guys ate in silence, taking care of their extreme hunger. On their second slice they started talking again.

Kevin decided to broach the subject that'd been hanging over them. Since D was along and he had his support, he went for it.

"So, how're things with your parents?" Kevin asked.

The weight of the world seemed to wash over Shin's face, and Kevin immediately regretted bringing it up.

"It's fine," Shin said, trying to brush it off.

Kevin looked at him skeptically. D flat out frowned.

"Dude," D countered, "you know that's not true."

"Really?" Shin shot back at D. "You're calling me out?"

"Yeah, man, I am. We talk about this every day. Don't you think you should tell Kevin, especially since he's so involved?"

"Shin, this impacts us so I think I should know what's going on," Kevin pleaded, both with his voice and expression.

"This is about their outdated ideas and you shouldn't have to worry about it." Shin's voice was full of frustration.

"Fine," Kevin said. "How do we date if your parents don't want us to? What kind of future could we possibly have?"

Kevin saw Shin's jaw tighten, his frustration starting to give way to anger. Kevin guessed this is how he must have looked when he lashed out at Quan earlier. He didn't like it but was determined to stand his ground.

It only lasted a moment. Shin's look softened and he took Kevin's hand. He let go a long sigh before he spoke.

"I love that you see a future for us. I'm glad my parents didn't totally scare you away. I've said it once before, and I'll say it again, I love you. It's only been a couple weeks, but I do."

Kevin squeezed Shin's hand.

"I love you, too, and I can stick it out to see what happens with your parents. But at least let me know what's going on, okay?"

They stared at each other until Shin broke the silence. "Alright. They ask every day if I've broken up with you. My mom, I think, is a little more open to the idea of us. You impressed her more than the other two guys I've brought home.

"Dad, on the other hand..." he sighed, shaking his head. "Won't budge. He's being very traditional about this and he's getting pressure from his father. I don't know why granddad's involved, but he is and they insist that my future husband be Japanese. That's right, dad calls this guy my husband. He's progressive like that, but there's a significance of dating someone Japanese. He assures me it'd be the same if we were discussing a woman. Like that's supposed to make me feel better."

Shin rolled his eyes and took a couple bites of pizza. Kevin waited for him to finish.

"So, like I said, this repeats every day. My dad says he's losing patience, but whatever. I'm not walking away from you."

"Is there anything I can do to help?"

"Just keep doing what you're doing," Shin said. "And I promise we'll talk more. You're right. We're in this together."

Kevin melted. Shin must have seen it in his face as his expression changed, too. Kevin wanted to hug him, but he couldn't from across the table. Instead he wrapped Shin's hand in both of his.

"I love you," Kevin said.

"I love you, too."

"Okay, enough of that," D said. "Some of us are trying to eat." He winked at them before he took a huge bite of his pizza.

NINE

Kevin was thrilled to be on a road trip with Shin, even if it was just across the river to the Meadowlands. D and Marshall were along, too, but as far as Kevin was concerned this was about being with Shin in the backseat. It was really cool to be sitting so close to Shin, but Kevin kept his impulses in check. He didn't want the straight boys up front to be uncomfortable with whatever was happening in the back.

The Meadowlands was hosting its first ever parkour competition. Shin and D wanted to compete, but they couldn't since they weren't eighteen. There were demo courses, however, and those were open to sixteen and older, so they would all get to try them instead. Kevin was excited to try out his skills somewhere new, especially since Shin and D were with him. He essentially had two coaches since D was more involved in his training. Ever since the incident with Quan, he'd grown closer to D and now considered him a good friend.

What was even better was Marshall and D were totally hitting it off. It was too bad they weren't gay as their budding bromance was in full bloom. Marshall had become a parkour fan. He was too scared to try some of the moves because of his football bulk, but he did scale the gym's rock wall a few times and enjoyed it. D, on the other hand, started playing catch with Marshall in the park while Shin and Kevin practiced on the rocks.

The parking lot was nearly full when they arrived, but luckily they snagged a spot. It was an outdoor event, and even from where they parked, they could see some of the courses that had been laid out. Kevin could make out people jumping up and down on some of them. He started to feel nervous about trying them out in front of a crowd.

Shin grabbed his arm to keep him moving. "Come on! Let's go!"

They walked quickly to the ticket area, Shin leading the way, excited to get inside.

"This is going to be mad cool!" Marshall said, looking at the vast array of things to try. "Can you run stuff like this yet, Kev?"

Kevin took it all in. "Some of this stuff looks insane. I've been doing pretty basic moves. You've seen most of them. But I'm willing to try something new."

"Hey, check this out," Shin said, once they'd gotten their tickets.

He led them to the far side of the event space where he'd discovered several short courses that hadn't been visible from the parking lot. Some were familiar to Kevin as they were similar to what he'd done at the gym or had seen on TV. The sign over the entrance to the area read "Test Zone."

"Cool," Kevin said.

As they drew closer, the layout of the Test Zone became more clear. There were individual items like the salmon ladder and cliffhanger, and some mini-*Ninja Warrior* courses with obstacles strung together. There was no shortage of parkour-focused courses, utilizing urban obstacles like scaffolding, dumpsters, light poles and park benches.

This was awesome. Kevin stopped, blown away by the possibilities. He missed Shin, Marshall and D passing him to go on into the zone.

Kevin felt anxious but excited. Tons of people were going through the courses with varying degrees of success. As one person successfully scaled a salmon ladder, two others struggled, one falling to the mats below. People were queued up to try the cliffhanger. Two guys, nearly as big as Marshall, scaled a cargo net. There was a huge line for the barrel roll, with some people around his age, and some a lot older.

"Come on in, don't be shy," said the guy at the entrance to the area. "You can try anything in here. Just get in the lines. If you go to the freestyling area, you get ninety seconds to do whatever you want."

The mix of ages and skill levels started to put him at ease and he came out of his daze. His friends were already in line for the sextuple steps.

"You were just going to leave me out there?" Kevin asked as he joined them.

"I told them you'd catch up once you'd processed it all," Marshall said. "I knew you needed a minute."

As they talked about strategy for the steps, the group shuffled positions and Kevin ended up at the front. Nerves hit him hard as he was about to go out there with everyone watching. People were wiping out on obstacles all around him, but he didn't want to be one of those people.

"Wait, how'd I end up going first?" He looked over at Shin, hoping he'd offer to go instead.

"Don't worry about it. Just go out there and show those steps who's boss." Shin grinned at him and Kevin had no choice but to proceed.

Kevin stepped onto the starting platform and studied the steps. Three to his left and three to the right, each step about five feet tall and angled to make them steep. It didn't look that hard, but he knew from watching that it was deceptive. Taking a deep breath, he approached the steps at jogging pace, he planted a foot on each step, going back and forth between his left and right. He was on the other side in no time.

Kevin's friends cheered.

Shin and D followed and made it through with no problem, each going faster than Kevin. That wasn't surprising.

Marshall didn't approach the steps with enough speed and it threw him off. He tripped on the third step, and face-planted on the side of the fourth before crashing to the mat below. He stood up, smiled and raised his arms over his head as if he'd succeeded.

"Damn it," Marshall said, rejoining the group. "Those steps need more padding." He sighed as he rubbed his jaw. "I really thought I had that. Oh well, at least the fall was spectacular."

Marshall laughed and everyone joined in, glad that he hadn't seriously injured himself.

"You weren't going fast enough," D said. "If you go too slow it's hard to find the rhythm."

"Now you tell me," Marshall said, smirking.

Kevin split away from the group as something grabbed his attention.

"I wanna try the cliffhanger," he called out while staring up at the monolith.

"Really?" Shin asked, joining Kevin.

"Yeah, man. After all the climbing you've had me doing, I want to put it to the test."

"Well we definitely want to do it, so let's go," D said.

As they waited, they carefully watched the people in front of them, trying to learn what and what not to do. The wall was about twenty feet long and fifteen feet high. The challenge was to traverse the obstacle using only your finger tips to grip the narrow strips of wood that formed a ledge. It wasn't a straight shot across though, there were gaps in the small ledge and sometimes the track moved up or down. On TV, Kevin had seen many people fail this. Yet, he was excited to try.

D was the first up and he fell at the second transition point. He lost his grip while trying to get the correct hand position. He cursed in Japanese as he fell. Kevin was starting to learn some Japanese, but only the curse words he heard frequently at the gym.

"You ready for this?" Shin asked.

"Sure. If I fall, I fall. This is hardcore. Hell, D fell and he's a lot better than me. I just want to see how far I can go."

"Go get 'em," Marshall said.

Kevin stepped up to the wall. The first section was easy to grab since he was tall. There was only an inch or so of ledge to hold on to. He found a grip that felt good, lifted his feet off the platform and started to work his way across.

He got past the first transition, where he had to reach and pull himself up to another level, putting his growing biceps to good use. His arms were starting to tingle, but weren't burning yet, so he continued. His lankiness served him well here as he had less size and weight to move. He couldn't imagine Marshall trying this.

"Keep going, Kevin," Shin said. "You're looking great."

To Kevin's surprise he was doing it and using his body pretty efficiently, maintaining his momentum without knocking himself off the wall. He was coming up to the point where D fell and that meant he was past half. His arms were killing him now and it felt like he had hot pins in his fingers. He applied the same mindset he used at track meets where he pushed his body to stay ahead of the competition.

It wasn't enough. His grip slipped at the transition and he dropped off the wall.

"Damn it," he said as he hit the air-filled mat that resembled something a stuntman might drop in to. He rolled off the mat and onto solid ground.

"You did great!" Shin yelled from his place at the starting position.

Even though he was a little disappointed, Kevin felt good about what he'd done. The first time on a real cliffhanger and he'd hung with D.

"Good job, man," D said as he came over and clapped Kevin on the back.

They watched as Shin approached the wall. He moved quick, barely slowing down at the transition points. He completed the obstacle in just under a minute. Shin and D bumped fists before he wrapped Kevin in a hug.

"I hope you know how good you did," Shin said, ignoring his own achievement. "That was really excellent."

"I'm thrilled," Kevin said while giving a giddy grin. "I think I know how to do better next time."

"You're doing it again?"

"Maybe later. My arms are spent."

They turned their attention to Marshall who was assessing his options at the start of the cliffhanger.

"Well look who it is," Quan said.

They turned and found Quan with three other guys, two Kevin recognized from the gym.

"It's so cute you're still trying to be together." Quan shook his head as if scolding a child. Two of his friends mirrored him.

"What are you doing here?" Shin asked, masking none of his annoyance. "You don't even like this stuff."

"These guys," Quan said, gesturing to the guys around him, "are competing and I wanted to cheer them on." Quan smiled, and it wasn't at all pleasant. "It's nice you're getting one last Saturday together before this comes to an end. And then you'll find out where your real future lies."

"Just go," D said, stepping up in front of Quan. "You're not welcome here."

"You better watch yourself, D, you might find yourself on the outs just like Red is."

"Come on, D," Shin said, tugging at his friend's shirt. "He's not worth..."

"You should listen to D," Marshall said as he moved past Kevin and Shin and placed himself next to D. He crossed his arms over his chest, which made him look even bigger.

The guys with Quan exchanged nervous glances while he remained defiant.

"Having the Hulk on your side changes nothing." If he was scared, he didn't let on. "Let's go, guys. See you later, Shin."

"Um, no. No, you won't," Shin called out as Quan and his friends turned and walked away.

"What's wrong with him?" Marshall asked.

"He's been tweaked as long as I've known him," D said, staring after Quan before finally turning back to the group.

"Sorry," Shin said. "I didn't expect to run into him here."

Kevin reached out and took Shin's hand. "It's okay. He's a dick. Whatever." He pulled Shin towards him so they stood closer together. "What do you think he meant by find out where your real future lies?"

"That's kinda creepy." Marshall said.

"No idea," Shin said. "He loves mind games and trying to control the situation."

"Let's forget about it, okay?" Kevin said. "Let's practice some more, grab lunch and watch the competition. Hopefully we won't run into him again."

"I wouldn't count on it," D muttered under his breath.

Shin nodded. "I'm in."

"Me too," said Marshall, putting his arm around D's shoulders.

"Sure," said D, his irritation relaxing into a smile. Marshall gave him an appreciative shake before releasing him.

"How'd you do on the cliffhanger anyway?" Kevin asked Marshall as they started walking. "I missed it."

"Didn't really get started. I saw what was happening and dropped to the mat so I could back up D."

"Want to give it another try?" Kevin asked.

"Nah. I was on it long enough to know that I shouldn't be doing that. I'm gonna climb the cargo net. That requires strength that I've got, but doesn't require balance or funky moves."

"Alright, cargo net it is," D said, leading the way.

TEN

"You're doing great at the gym," Shin said as they exited the subway and headed towards Kevin's apartment after working out. "It's like you've had a breakthrough over the past couple of days. Your agility is way up, you're flipping much better and there's more confidence in your moves."

"Seeing the pros last weekend was inspirational."

"You're also looking good." Shin squeezed Kevin's bicep through his shirt as he exaggerated the words. "Have you noticed how you're bulking up? Only a few weeks and look at you."

Kevin blushed. He'd noticed. There was definition in his chest and arms that hadn't been there before. There was still a long way to go before he could compare yet to Shin or D, but he liked what he saw in the mirror. More than just a pole now.

"Yeah. I like it."

"So do I," Shin said, leaning in and whispering in his ear.

"Uh-Oh." Kevin said, not getting to respond to Shin's flirting.

"Shit," Shin said, watching Quan come towards them on the crowded sidewalk. "Maybe he'll pass us by."

"Really? You know that's not going to happen. But I like your

67

optimism." Kevin smiled, even though he knew it would be short-lived.

"Shin, Red," Quan said, sharply. He stopped, holding them up as there was no easy way to get past him given the bustling people around them.

"Don't you dare call him that," Shin said. "If you can't be nice, you'll at least be respectful."

Kevin liked being stood up for, even though he could certainly speak for himself.

"Whatever," Quan said dismissively. "You still crashing with D or have you found somewhere else? Maybe with your boyfriend, or whatever you're calling him these days?"

Crashing with D? Kevin worked hard to keep the surprise off his face. He wanted to make sure Quan didn't realize that he was unaware of this new development.

"Where I'm staying is none of your business. Come on, Kevin." Shin squeezed Kevin's hand and tried to move around Quan.

Quan stayed in front of them, blocking their path.

"I'm sure my family would be happy to take you in until everything's worked out."

"Hey guys, what's going on?" Marshall stepped up next to Shin. Kevin was thrilled with his friend's excellent timing. "This pipsqueak bothering you guys again?"

"Does Red know everything?" Quan didn't acknowledge Marshall.

"Yeah, I do," Kevin said, lying. Quan wasn't going to get the satisfaction of seeing Kevin get angry, this time not only at Quan but Shin, too.

Marshall repeated his move from last weekend and stepped between Quan and the couple. "Why are you bothering these guys again? I thought D and I were clear." Marshall's tone was chilling, and left no room for discussion.

"Well, I just..." Quan couldn't ignore him now.

"You just what?"

"But... I..."

"Go. Now."

Quan said nothing else, but peered around Marshall to look at Shin, who glared back. Marshall remained immovable. Quan eventually turned around and took off.

"Wow. The power of having huge friends," Shin said, as they started moving down the sidewalk again.

"What was all that about?" Marshall asked. "You're not living at home?"

"Yeah," Kevin said, his annoyance quickly surfacing, "what was that?"

Shin opened his mouth, closed it and then opened it again, but no words came out.

"Unbelievable," Kevin said, ripping his hand out of Shin's grip and leaving him and Marshall behind.

"Kevin, wait."

Kevin wasn't waiting. He didn't like being lied to. Even if it was a lie of omission. He still asked every day how things were at home and the answer was always the same. Clearly something had changed and Shin was keeping it to himself.

Shin jogged to catch up to Kevin and matched his pace.

"Let's talk."

"Sure, you want to talk now, after I hear the news from the worst possible source. How long have you been at D's?"

"A couple days." Shin's toned changed. It was more apologetic, ashamed that he'd been caught.

"Really?" Kevin seethed now that he had more of the details.

"I didn't..."

"You didn't think getting thrown out was something I'd want to know?"

"I wasn't thrown out," Shin said, sounding proud of himself. "I left. I didn't want to hear any more from my father."

"So you ran away?" Kevin couldn't believe what he was hearing.

He thought Shin was smarter than that. "That doesn't solve anything."

"It shows how serious I am."

"I imagine he doesn't see it that way." Kevin didn't stop at the stairs up to his building. He continued right up to the door.

"I can explain."

"For lying or making things worse?"

Kevin unlocked the door and stepped in, but turned to block Shin. Marshall hung back, waiting by the stoop of the building next door. Kevin appreciated him keeping his distance.

"No. Not right now. I need to think."

"Can I call you later?"

"I'll call you when I figure this out."

Kevin closed the door leaving Shin outside. Once upstairs, he slammed the apartment door and headed for his room. How could Shin do that? How could D let Shin keep this from him?

Kevin flopped back on his bed when he heard the apartment door open and close. He watched the doorway, waiting for Marshall to appear.

"Can I come in or do you need some time?" he asked, leaning against the doorframe. Kevin propped his head up on his hand and gave a weak smile. "I can't believe he kept that from you," Marshall continued. "But I thought you knew, by the way you acted."

"No way I was going to let Quan know that *I* didn't know." Kevin paused, tapping his fingers on the bed. "Sorry you saw the fallout. But I'm glad if it was anyone, that it was you. At least you're not going to go babbling about it to everyone."

Marshall nodded. "So, what are you going to do?"

"I have no idea. I mean, this is a big deal, right?"

"It's too bad his parents can't support you guys. You said Shin's close to them, so he can't be happy."

"But..."

"Come on, man, let me finish. You asked for my opinion."

"Sorry. Go on."

Marshall came all the way into the room and sat on the stool at the work table.

"Clearly you've won out over his parents. He left home because he's that into you. That says something about his feelings. Here's what I don't get. You guys are sixteen. It's not like you're getting married tomorrow, or even in a year. Why is it such a big deal who he's dating now?"

Marshall was right, it didn't make sense. Yes, Shin's parents demanded that he date only Japanese guys, and Quan seemed to be fanning the flames. But why did it all matter now? As much as Kevin and Shin had said the words "future," there was no sure sign yet that this was long term. Kevin eventually shrugged.

"Going back to something you can control, did you make the right choice by sending him away? He's fighting for you guys."

"He lied and he ran away from home. Shouldn't I have some say in what's happening?"

"I think you've said a lot. You crushed him when you left him outside."

Kevin frowned, let himself fall back onto the bed and stared blankly at the ceiling.

"You think I'm wrong?"

Marshall sighed. "Sorry, but, yeah, I do. Look, if you two break up who's to say he doesn't fall for another white guy, or a latino or someone else who isn't what his parents want?"

Kevin sat up and crossed his legs under him.

"I guess I'm screwed no matter what. Neither of us can be truly happy with this hanging over our heads."

"I wish I had a way to fix it."

"It's okay. You make sense, though."

Marshall looked at his watch and stood up.

"I gotta get home. Stuff to do before dinner. You gonna be okay?"

"Yeah. I've got homework to keep me occupied."

"Call him?"

"Maybe."

Marshall headed for the door.

"Hey man, thanks."

"Anytime."

Kevin sprawled across the bed as Marshall let himself out.

Kevin hadn't considered the possibility that Shin could easily end up with another guy his parents didn't like. If that was the case, why should Kevin give up so easily and be the one to break up the relationship? Especially since Shin was willing to defy his parents just to be with him. Shin's lack of honesty really bothered him, though. If he was capable of keeping a secret this big, what might Shin hide in the future?

Kevin needed time to figure this out. And it was going to take more than just sleeping on it. His heart loved Shin, but was it enough to overrule his head warning him not to get mixed up in this drama.

ELEVEN

"WHAT ARE WE DOING HERE?" Marshall asked as they arrived at the rocks in Central Park. "With Shin grounded, it's not like you're going run into him."

"We're here because I don't want to start losing my new skills. I need to get some practice in, even if it's without a coach."

Shin's grounding sucked. It was another layer of complication. Kevin got a text from D with the details. Shin was forced back home shortly after his blow up with Kevin. Now he was grounded indefinitely. He was only allowed to go to school and school-related activities. Otherwise he was restricted to home. When he was home, his phone was locked up and he could only use the internet in the living room where he could be watched.

"If you can't date him, any chance you guys could just be friends? Like with D? Shin's a cool guy and it'd be a shame not to..." Marshall stopped, seeing the look on his friend's face.

Kevin dropped his pack on the ground and stripped off his shirt. He'd gotten a little bit of color, so he wasn't his usual pasty self, and he wanted to keep that, too.

"Do you know something you're not telling me?"

"D texted me. And no I haven't been hiding it from you," Marshall sounded defensive, a tone he didn't usually take with Kevin. "I got it during lunch and this is the first time I've seen you since this morning."

"Okay. Okay." Kevin raised his hands in surrender. "I shouldn't be so suspicious."

"D misses us. He was wondering if we could hang out. The three of us, or the four of us. We'd planned on going to a Rangers game tomorrow before all this new stuff happened. He wanted to make sure we were still on."

"What'd you tell him?"

"I said we were. There's no reason I can't be friends with D, is there?"

Kevin paused, perhaps too long, and then finally shook his head.

"Of course you can."

"Good. That was the right answer." Marshall smiled, which lightened Kevin's mood. He didn't like talking about this. The separation from Shin hurt too much. "D would love to stay friends with you, too. But, he knows that's a lot more difficult given where things are."

Kevin started doing some warm up moves and stretches.

"From what D knows," Marshall continued, "Shin's dad is just digging in. He's sure Shin'll give in soon since he's grounded. His dad somehow knows you sent Shin away, and he thinks that's a turning point."

"So glad I was able to help," Kevin said, wishing he'd added even more sarcasm.

"Don't go beating yourself up. It's not worth it."

"I suppose I should be flattered he's holding his ground."

"He wants you. D said Shin sees that as the only victory."

Kevin didn't want to talk any more. Instead, he focused on jumping up on one of the rocks and then jumping between them, finding a good pace. He enjoyed going through the motions and stretching his limbs. Marshall sat down, taking his usual spot on the grass.

Kevin went to where he and Shin usually started runs. He jumped up on the boulder, and moved into a handstand which morphed into a flip that landed him on the ground in a standing position.

"Nice!" Marshall said, excited. "Well done."

Kevin continued to move over and around the rocks. After he did a front flip off a rock, he ran straight for one of the trees. He wasn't good at flipping off trees yet, but he went for it. He ran up the tree three steps but didn't hit the last step right. The flip came up short and he missed the landing, his shoulder and head hitting the ground hard.

Too hard. Pain tore through his body.

He grunted only once before he blacked out.

TWELVE

KEVIN FELT like he'd been run over by a truck. Everything ached, from head to toe. Without opening his eyes, he started to test out his body to see if he could move. He was able to flex his fingers and toes, though the later caused his legs to cramp up a little. He tried to reposition his legs but that only made things worse. He could move his left arm, but not his right, which seemed to be restrained in some way. Finally, summoning up some courage, he opened his eyes.

Kevin felt a little disoriented as his eyes slowly adjusted to his surroundings. He was in bed, the rails on either side giving away that he was in a hospital. The last thing he remembered was being in the park with Marshall. What happened? He looked around the room. There were a lot of tubes and machines hooked up to him. It was getting dark outside. Next to the window was Shin, asleep in a chair. He didn't look comfortable with his chin down on his chest and his hands gripping the chair arms, as if he might fall out if he didn't hold on.

"Shin." He said it so quietly he could barely hear himself. His mouth was so dry. Even the whisper hurt.

He tried again. He needed to know where he was, how he got here and why Shin was the only one in the room with him.

"Shin," he said again. It sounded like a croak but it was louder this time. Shin jerked awake and in a single movement was at his bedside.

"Kevin! You're awake. Thank God. I'll get your parents."

Shin darted from the room before Kevin could say anything. He quickly returned with a nurse.

"Marshall and D went to the cafeteria to get your parents. They'll be here soon."

Shin stayed by the door while the nurse checked the monitors and Kevin.

"It's nice to have you with us," she said, making some notes on her iPad. "We've called one of your doctors and he'll be along in a few minutes." She placed a call light in his hand.

Kevin gripped it tightly, as if it were the most precious thing in the world. She re-filled the water pitcher from his bedside table with fresh water and poured some into a plastic cup.

"You can have water," she said, dropping a straw into the cup. "Take small sips at a time. You don't want to go too fast, okay?"

Kevin nodded. She put the cup on the table and wheeled it around so that it crossed his bed, making it easy to reach with his left hand.

The nurse took some additional notes, and checked his eyes and temperature.

"I'll be back soon. Push the button if you need anything, okay?"

"Okay," he finally said.

He watched her leave the room and then focused on Shin who hadn't moved.

"What happened?" Kevin rasped.

Shin moved into the room, but hesitantly. Kevin put the call light down next to him and reached for the water. His hand started to tremble as he picked it up and some of it spilled onto the sheets. Shin quickly stepped up beside him, putting his hand around Kevin's to steady the cup.

"Let me."

Shin guided the cup back down to the table, allowing Kevin to pull his hand away. Shin picked up the cup and held it to make the straw easily accessible. Kevin took the straw between his lips and sucked up a little water. He let the cold liquid sit on his tongue and wet the inside of his mouth for a moment before swallowing. He took several small sips, each one more eager than the last.

"Thanks," he said, finally pulling away from the straw. He sounded more like himself now.

He saw tears welling up in Shin's eyes as he set the cup on the table. Kevin reached out, grabbed Shin's hand and held it lightly.

"What happened?" Kevin asked, again.

He didn't know what to make of Shin's tears.

"You were practicing at the rocks. Marshall was watching. You tried to flip off the tree, something went wrong. You hit your head pretty bad and banged up your right shoulder."

That explained why he couldn't move that arm. It was still under the sheet out of sight, and it was too much trouble to pull it out and get a look.

"You've been here for four days," Shin continued.

"No way, you mean it's..." Kevin thought about what day it would be "...Monday?"

Shin nodded.

"Oh my God," Kevin said very quietly. His grip on Shin's hand tightened as the gravity of the situation sunk in.

"I hope it's okay I'm here," Shin said, his voice cracking as the tears started to fall. "Your parents have been here the whole time, they just stepped out to eat. Marshall and D have been here a lot, too. I know I'm probably the last person you wanted to wake up to."

"Stop."

It was a lot of information to take in and his mind struggled to process it. He remembered practicing in the park, but didn't remember anything going wrong. He knew one thing for certain. He was happy that Shin was here.

"I love..."

"Kevin, thank god you're awake," his mom said as she swooped into the room. His dad was close behind. They stood on the opposite side of the bed from Shin. Kevin's mom ran her fingers through his hair, as if trying to comfort him.

"I'll let you all talk," Shin said as he tried to slip from Kevin's grip.

Kevin's eyes shifted over to Shin. He gave Shin's hand an extra squeeze but didn't let him go.

"Stay," Kevin said.

"I'll just be in the waiting room," Shin said, gently extracting his hand from Kevin's grasp.

"Have you seen a doctor yet?" Kevin's dad asked as Kevin's eyes followed Shin, watching him slowly leave the room.

"No," Kevin said softly. "The nurse called one."

"How do you feel?" his mom asked.

Kevin considered for a moment.

"Stiff. Sore. I hurt all over."

"You scared us pretty good," his dad said, "and especially Marshall, since he saw it happen."

A doctor walked in with the nurse who'd been in earlier.

"It is great to see you awake," the doctor said, smiling at Kevin before turning to his parents. "We need to perform some tests. Mr. and Mrs. McCollum, I'm sorry to send you out already, but we need to run him through some neuro checks. Then we're going to take him for a scan to see how his brain looks now that he's awake."

"Of course," Kevin's mom said. "We'll be outside with your friends."

His mom leaned over and kissed his forehead.

"We'll come back as soon as you're done," his dad said just before closing the door.

The doctor ran Kevin through several tests, which he passed with flying colors. After they were finished, he was assisted into a wheelchair and pushed out into the hallway. He saw his parents in the nearby waiting room smiling and waving as he was wheeled by. Marshall and D were there, too, looking very much relieved. Kevin's heart sank. Shin wasn't with them.

The tests seemed to last forever, made worse by Shin's absence. They kept sending him in and out of the scanner, asking him to turn his head slowly, first to the left, and then to the right. It was frustrating. And the technician wouldn't say anything about the results, her expression blank.

Finally, Kevin was returned to his room. Once he was back in bed, the nurse helped him sit up. His body still hurt so he hoped the new position would help, making it easier to drink and get a better view of the room without having to twist his body too much.

It was nearly nine on Monday night. He should be at home doing homework. Not here. Here was the last place he wanted to be. Kevin wanted everything to go back to normal, and as quickly as possible. He was glad, at least, that his shoulder wouldn't screw up track, because the season was already over. But, it might ruin his parkour training for good.

He laid back and closed his eyes, the thought of it was all so overwhelming. He needed to know exactly how bad this was. Was it just a broken shoulder? Or was there something more? And, Shin's absence still weighed heavily on his mind.

There was a knock at the door. He opened his eyes and saw Marshall standing in the doorway.

"Hey," Kevin said.

"Dude, you scared the shit out of me."

"Sorry, man. I think I know how you feel when you get hit on the field now. I have a new respect for what you do out there."

Marshall smiled as he moved towards the bedside.

"What happened to Shin? I didn't see him..." Kevin's voice trailed off.

"He had to go. He had to get home before his parents did. He's been here when he could sneak away. He's still grounded."

Kevin sighed, a little relieved. "When I woke up, for a moment when I saw him, I'd forgotten everything that'd happened. Then it all came flooding back, that I don't get to..." Kevin yawned.

Marshall put his hand on his friend's good shoulder. "Don't think about it right now. You need to rest so you can get outta here. It's no fun hanging with you in here. For starters the cable's complete crap. No bad sci-fi anywhere."

Kevin laughed, then winced at the pain it caused.

"I'll see you tomorrow after school, okay?"

Kevin nodded.

"Your parents will be in soon. They were talking to the doctor when I came back."

"Thanks, Marshall."

"Anytime, man."

Marshall was barely out of the room before Kevin's eyes drooped and he fell asleep.

THIRTEEN

KEVIN GOT out of the hospital Thursday and went back to school, at his insistence, on Friday. His parents wanted him to stay home and go back on Monday, but he'd missed enough and didn't want to get any further behind.

Luckily the workload wasn't as crazy as he thought it'd be, and the teachers were lenient on deadlines. Apparently a hospital stay with broken bones and mild concussion got you a lot of sympathy.

Marshall jumped down the front steps of the school to meet Kevin, who was perched on the railing, reading his lit book.

"Shall I hail a cab for you, sir?" Marshall asked, sounding like a butler with a really bad British accent.

"I'm not an invalid," Kevin said emphatically. "Mom's not here, so I say we're walking. Taking a cab this morning was ridiculous."

Marshall laughed. He'd gotten an earful earlier in the day about taking a cab because Kevin didn't want special treatment. He wanted things to go back to normal and part of that was taking his usual walk through Central Park. Kevin glared at his friend, obviously annoyed.

"How're you feeling?" Marshall asked, changing topics.

"I'm okay. A little tired, but not bad," Kevin stood and dropped the book in his pack, which he slung over his good shoulder. He headed toward the park and Marshall followed. "The sling is uncomfortable and awkward. It sure makes writing a bitch. I'm going to have to learn how to write with my left hand."

They cut a direct path across the park, going no where near the rocks. Kevin certainly couldn't practice, and he didn't even want to see them right now. They avoided talking about Shin and the accident, focusing instead on Marshall's date with Cassie tomorrow.

"You wanna grab a bite before we hit the books?" Marshall asked when they were just a couple blocks from home.

They shared chemistry class and it was the subject Kevin was the most behind in, more so than any of the others. While they both did okay in class, Marshall seemed to be better at it, especially the formulas which always gave Kevin trouble. They hoped to get all the studying knocked out that night to keep the rest of the weekend free.

"What if we hit Fairway and stock up on munchies? We're gonna be up late anyway, we might as well pig out while we're doing it."

"Sounds..." Marshall stopped talking and gripped Kevin's arm so he'd stop. "You've got a visitor."

Shin sat on Kevin's stoop. He was wearing earbuds and his head was buried in a textbook. He hadn't noticed them yet.

Kevin's stomach summersaulted. He was thrilled to see Shin, but was worried what the visit might mean.

"I'll get the food," Marshall said, "and hang at my place. Text me when you're done."

Kevin hung back a little as Marshall walked ahead. Shin looked up as he passed by and they exchanged nods before Shin looked back towards Kevin. Their eyes locked and Shin quickly stood up, pulling out his earbuds.

Kevin slowly walked toward him as if he were heading toward his doom.

"Hey," Shin said. The sadness in Shin's voice pulled on Kevin's heart strings.

"Hey Shin, it's good to see you." Kevin tried to sound confident, though he was far from it.

"D told me you were out of the hospital." They stared at each other for a moment before Shin continued. "How's the shoulder?"

"Pain in the ass is what this is." Kevin jerked his sling a bit for emphasis. "You still grounded?" It was a lame question, but it was all he had.

Shin nodded. "Probably going to have something else taken away today since I should be at home. But I had to see you. There's a lot of stuff going on, more than I realized. And I want you to know about it."

"Come on up," Kevin said as he went up the stairs to unlock the door. Even though he knew he shouldn't, he took Shin's hand as they entered and went upstairs.

Kevin opened the apartment and led them into the kitchen. He wanted to keep the conversation somewhere neutral rather than in his personal space. If this was going to be a breakup, he didn't want that memory in his room.

"Have a seat," Kevin said, gesturing to one of the stools at the kitchen island.

Shin sat down as Kevin took a seat on the other side, directly across from Shin.

"I'm sorry this got so crazy," Shin started before Kevin could say anything. "Remember I told you I hadn't expected there to be any trouble bringing you home. It caught me by surprise. In the last few days, though, I've learned a lot about my family. Some of it I'm still thinking about. It's just so unbelievable."

"Tell me." Kevin said. He didn't expect he'd like anything he was about to hear, especially given how grave Shin sounded.

"Quan's played a huge role in this, manipulating things behind the scenes. I don't think *all* of it's him, but I'm sure he's the reason why my parents won't listen to me."

Kevin shook his head. Unbelievable was right.

"Remember when he talked about finding where my true future lies?" Shin asked.

"Yeah. It made him sound like a stalker."

"Exactly. And his family wanting to take me in. They've always been nosy, but this was way beyond the usual."

Shin sighed again and Kevin resisted the urge to take his hand. Shin needed to lay out the situation on his own. There was a long silence while Shin collected his thoughts.

"This goes way back to when my parents first met. They were part of an *o-miai*, or arranged marriage. They were matched when they were only fifteen. They both came to this country to attend NYU and they married right after graduation. But, the story I've always heard was that they met and fell in love as freshmen and dated through college before getting married." Shin paused, letting it sink in. "They don't really talk about it because *o-miai* isn't really understood in this country."

"Arranged marriages still happen?" Kevin was surprised.

"It's the way almost all marriages used to be. It's been on the decline for decades, but it wasn't unheard of when my parents did it, and it's still possible today. Mom and dad were arranged because their parents wanted to mix the family assets. It was very old school. The same thing happened with my mom's older brother."

"Was this a good thing?"

Shin shrugged. "For my mom and dad it's been good. They really do love each other. She confirmed that for me. And they fell for each other pretty quickly at NYU which made the marriage easy."

"She confirmed it? You've talked to her?"

"Yeah. Yesterday. But dad's not having any of it. No discussion, at all. He just wants me to do exactly what he says. He even put more restrictions on me after visiting you in the hospital. But, mom told me she likes you."

Shin smiled a little, and Kevin couldn't help but smile back.

"Mom also watched her brother go through a miserable marriage that lasted twenty years. She thinks the pressure is coming from my father's father. He wants a proper selection made and wants my father to take care of it. My granddad would rather it be a girl, but has come to understand that it will be a boy. And since I'm already a year older than my dad when his marriage was arranged, the pressure's amped up."

Kevin nodded.

"What?" Shin looked perplexed.

"At least there's some reasoning behind everything. Marshall was asking the other day what the big deal was since you and I were still in high school and it wasn't like we were asking to get married. At least I understand now, and why it blindsided you."

"I still don't get. O-miai seems so ancient even in my parents' time. And today, really? Don't get me wrong, Kevin, I love you. I want to date you, get to know you, teach you more parkour and have fun. Do I want to commit to marrying you, right now? No." It hurt Shin to say no, even though it was true.

"Don't worry," Kevin said. "I'm not ready to say yes to marriage either. We've only known each other a few weeks. Who knows what happens as we get older and head off to college."

"I'm glad we agree on that."

"So did your dad say who he wants to marry you off to? Or is it that it just has to be someone Japanese?"

Shin ran a hand through his thick hair, leaving it with a tussled look that Kevin liked.

"Quan," Shin said quietly.

"What?" Kevin was stupefied. Shin's parents had to know why those two broke up. Why would they try to put Shin back with him?

"Right?" Shin said. "I almost laughed at dad when he told me."

"What on earth does Quan have that would make marrying him worthwhile?"

"Apparently he's got family high up in the Kyoto government and my grandfather would love to see our family tied to theirs. Quan's grandfather is all for it, and so are his parents. To them, I'm a catch because of my smarts, plus my parents have solid professions and my grandparents have status as well. But, I made it clear that I wouldn't be marrying Quan under any circumstance because I don't like him."

"This is crazy," Kevin said. "So Quan helped manufacture this whole thing?"

"Yeah. Once he found out that my parents wanted me to date only Japanese guys, he talked to his grandfather which got the ball rolling. His grandfather talked to my grandfather. Soon enough, my dad was on board, seeing it as a way to fix everything. I've made it clear that *ren'ai kekkon*, a marriage of love, is the only way I'm going and that it won't be happening for a long time. I really can't imagine marriage before I'm done with undergrad."

"Where did that leave things with your dad?"

"I don't know. *I have much to consider.*" Shin deepened his voice with an accent that sounded sort of like his father. "When I talked to mom she said he's conflicted. He's torn between what his father wants and what I want. If I had to guess, I'm not going to have to marry Quan, but I am going to have to date someone Japanese to please my dad. My mom's more open to someone who is non-Japanese, but she said it's not her first choice. When I came out, and it was a non-issue, I thought they were completely liberal, but apparently there's a strong traditional streak in them, too."

Kevin finally had a clear picture of what was going on, but was at a loss on what to do next.

"You're quiet," Shin said after some time had passed.

"I don't know what to say. But, I'm glad you told me everything."

Kevin got up and pulled two bottles of water from the fridge. He placed one on the counter in front of Shin and screwed the top off the other. Rather than sitting, he stood across the counter from Shin.

"Unfortunately, knowing everything doesn't change *anything*," Kevin said after taking a drink. "Your parents aren't going to let us date. I'm sure Quan would make sure we couldn't sneak around even if we wanted to, which I don't."

"We're breaking up, aren't we?" Shin asked, sounding like he'd been sucker punched.

Kevin wanted so badly to fix this, but he couldn't see how. The look on Shin's face was heartbreaking. Kevin looked at the counter, wishing a better answer laid in its granite surface.

"I don't know what else to do," Kevin said, as he looked back at Shin.

Shin gave Kevin's hand a final squeeze before he pulled back. The sad smile almost pushed Kevin to tears.

"Can we still be friends?"

"Maybe. Eventually. But not right now. I've got to get past not being able to be your boyfriend."

Shin nodded. "I understand. I'm not sure I could do it either."

He stood up, leaving his water unopened on the counter. He went quickly for the door before Kevin could show him out. Kevin slammed his fist down on the counter. He stood there for a while trying to collect his emotions before texting Marshall. It wasn't going to be easy to tell him what just went down.

FOURTEEN

KEVIN WAS at his desk reading *Death of a Salesman* for lit class. He wasn't enjoying anything about the evening's study time.

He hated reading at the desk. Unless he had to take notes, he preferred reading in bed, leaning against the headboard. With the sling though, he couldn't hold the book in two hands, and the text-book was too heavy to hold with just one.

While the story was good, it was very depressing. Under normal circumstances he would've enjoyed this play, but with Shin and the bad shoulder weighing him down, he wished he could skip ahead to something like *The Time Machine* or *Fahrenheit 451*, which were coming up soon in the sci-fi and social commentary module. Even though there were some serious messages in those books, at least they had a futuristic side to them.

Kevin dropped a pen into the book so he wouldn't lose his place and stared out the window in front of him. There wasn't much to see. It was nearly dark, the grayness punctuated by the light from the windows in the building across the street and the cars on the street.

He moved from the desk to the work table. The planetary base he'd been working on lay there looking like a construction site where the project had suddenly been scrapped. Stray Tinkertoys were scattered across the desk, at odds with his usual tidiness. They'd been that way for a few weeks, since just before he stopped seeing Shin.

Kevin smiled at the memory. Shin and X were going to see a movie called *M3: That Black Steel*, which was playing at an anime festival downtown. Shin knew Kevin was into sci-fi and asked if he'd like to tag along. It was the first time Kevin had ever seen Japanese animation and he loved it. Then, the next day, everything started falling apart.

The smile quickly faded. The memories were not helping his mood.

He picked up two pieces from the desk and, holding the rod in his right hand, he tried to attach it to the spool in his left. The position of the sling made it nearly impossible to do even this simple task. It seemed Tinkertoys were not a one-handed building material. He put away the rods and spools so the worktable would be orderly.

He pulled a tray of Legos towards him. Even though he could snap them together with only one hand, he wasn't feeling inspired to build.

"This is ridiculous," he said to the empty room as he put the tray back where it belonged.

He hadn't been in a funk like this when Javier moved away. Maybe because they had made the most of the time they had together, and making sure they had said their goodbyes before he moved across the country. Even though Kevin barely knew Shin, it felt like his heart had been ripped out and stomped on.

His mind wandered back to some of his favorite sci-fi stories. Maybe he was just trapped in the wrong timeline, and he needed to find his way back to the one where he and Shin were still together.

Maybe his feelings for Shin were getting magnified by the stress of his current condition. He looked down at his sling in irritation. There was probably an alternate timeline fix for that, too. Maybe he could find the right combination of Legos to build a time machine and set things right.

"Ha!" he said, mildly amused at his wishful thinking.

He grabbed his phone off the desk and called Marshall. This was something else Kevin hated. He didn't like talking on the phone. He preferred texting, but doing it one-handed produced a lot of auto-correct garbage.

"Kev! What's up?" Marshall was in mid-laugh as he picked up.

"Hey Kevin," Cassie said in the background.

"Oh hey," Kevin said, trying to not sound as down as he was. "I didn't realize you were hanging with Cassie."

"Yeah, decided to study at her place tonight. She's been cracking me up with her dramatic readings of *Comedy of Errors*. Been kinda hard getting any studying done."

It wasn't lost on Kevin that Cassie was getting to study something light, while he was wading through one of the saddest things he'd ever read. Didn't quite seem fair that the happier person was reading the comedy.

"You wanna come over?" Marshall asked.

"Nah. That's okay. I don't wanna get in the way."

"I wouldn't invite you if it wasn't okay."

"I know."

"It's cool, Kevin," Cassie said. "You can join us for some bad Shakespeare."

"Kevin, you okay?" Marshall asked, in more of a quiet voice.

Even over the phone, Kevin couldn't hide his feelings from his best friend.

"I'm just a little stir crazy, and I've decided to throw myself a pity party."

"I'll come over. Gimme fifteen minutes."

"Absolutely not," Kevin said, sternly. "I know Cassie would let you come over, but honestly I'll feel worse knowing I busted up your night because I'm feeling sorry for myself. It'd be one thing if you were just upstairs, alone, but you're not, and you're not going to leave her because I'm being stupid."

"Are you sure? It's in my job description to help you get through a breakup."

"But, I can't let you walk away from your girl for no good reason, and that's part of mine." Kevin said, truly meaning it.

"Okay. If you change your mind, you're welcome to drop by. I'm probably going to hang here for another couple hours. I guarantee she can make you laugh with these readings she's busting out. Or, if you need me there..."

"Got it. Now, hang up and be with your girlfriend."

"Alright. I'll stop by when I get home."

"Cool. See you then." Kevin hung up and leaned back in his chair.

He decided a change of scene was in order. Pocketing his phone, he grabbed his wallet and keys from the desk and walked into the hallway. He stopped in the living room where his mom and dad were watching TV.

"I'm gonna go for a walk, if that's alright," he said. "I'll be back in an hour or so."

"Everything okay?" dad asked.

"Yeah. Just want to clear my head."

They were up to date on what was going on with Shin, so they knew he had a lot on his mind.

"Alright," dad said.

"Can we talk you into picking up some OJ and some coffee pods?" mom asked.

"Yeah, sure."

"Just take a twenty out of my purse. Pick yourself up something, too, if you want."

He smiled a little. The injury kept him from doing a lot of things, but eating wasn't one of them. He suspected there might be ice cream in his future.

He nodded. "See you later."

He took his time, wandering aimlessly along Amsterdam Avenue. It was a pretty quiet evening, as it was a weeknight and rush hour was long since over. There were a few people out, but not enough to distract him as he window shopped, walked and thought.

He was glad to be outside as an early evening shower had cleared the air somewhat. It made it a little easier to think. He knew he wasn't coping well between the stuff with Shin and his busted shoulder making him lose his focus. Maybe the ice cream would help, he thought, and he laughed just a little bit.

Kevin had been gone almost half an hour when he entered Fairway. He quickly picked up the orange juice and coffee for his mom before heading to the freezer section. He placed the basket at his feet. Choosing the right flavor of ice cream was serious business, and would take some time.

"Can't I go anywhere without running into you?"

"Shit." Kevin mouthed the word. He saw Quan's reflection in the glass, standing behind him.

"Not exactly something I enjoy either." Kevin didn't turn to face him. He stayed focused on the ice cream selection, hoping Quan would take the hint.

"You must be proud of yourself."

What the hell did that mean? Quan's reflection grew larger as he took a step closer. He looked annoyed and angry, angrier than Kevin had ever seen him before.

"Look. It's over. We broke up a few days ago. I'm sure you've heard all about it." Kevin finally turned to face Quan since, as usual, he wouldn't just go away. "I don't want to deal with any of your crap, so I'm just gonna go."

Kevin turned back, pulled a carton of peanut butter cup ice cream from the freezer and dropped it in the basket. He picked it up and started to make his way towards checkout.

Quan grabbed Kevin's arm as he walked away. He squeezed it so hard that Kevin dropped the basket.

"I'm not finished..." Quan started.

"What the hell?" Kevin went from annoyed to angry lightning

fast. He turned on Quan, ready to land a punch to his face. Quan let go of Kevin, his stance suggesting he was ready to fight.

"What are you boys doing? Take it outside." It was a security guard. Kevin was so focused on Quan that he didn't even see him coming.

"He came up on me and tried to take my stuff," Kevin said, pointing to the shopping basket. "Made me drop it."

"I did not," Quan said. "He's lying."

"Buy your stuff and get out of here," the guard said to Kevin.

Kevin wasn't going to argue, he grabbed the basket and left Quan behind.

"Are you buying anything?" Kevin heard the guard ask Quan.

"Um. Still looking."

Kevin didn't wait around to hear the rest. He got in the shortest line hoping to get out of there fast. As he waited, he thought about Quan's words. It didn't make any sense. What did he have to be proud of?

Even though Kevin hurried home, there was still time to make a few decisions. While he couldn't go running yet, he could at least walk the loop in the park every morning to get some exercise. He'd also start building again, at least with the Legos until he could use both arms. He thought if he could stay busy, doing things he enjoyed, he'd have less time to get into a mood. It wasn't who he was and he didn't want to let himself turn into that person either.

Kevin hated running into Quan, but at least the encounter had spurred him into action.

FIFTEEN

KEVIN WAS MORE terrified than he'd been on their first date. Shin texted him the night before, inviting him to dinner, at his place, with his parents. It'd been a couple weeks since they'd last talked, but something had definitely changed. After the shock wore off, he texted back that he would be there at six as requested. When he asked for more detail, Shin said he didn't have any, only that his parents asked him to make the invitation.

Kevin immediately texted D to see if he knew anything, but the invite surprised him as well. Kevin liked the he could ask D stuff like that. Since the accident, he and Marshall had been hanging out with D more and they'd all grown closer. Kevin hoped he'd be able to do the same with Shin one day.

Kevin now stood in front of his mirror, in a state of panic. He'd never stressed so much over what to wear, desperate to make a good impression. He changed shirts at least five times, which his healing shoulder didn't appreciate. Finally he settled on a light blue button down and dark jeans. He passed on the dress shoes, choosing a pair of smart, black sneakers. He considered a tie, but in the end decided against it. He didn't want it to look like he was trying too hard.

Kevin made good time getting to Shin's place and walked around the block once because he didn't want to seem too early. Once it was a couple minutes to six, he buzzed the intercom.

"Hello, Kevin," said Shin's mom, her face filling the screen. "Come on up."

She sounded much less stressed this time around, which Kevin hoped was a good sign. The door buzzed and Kevin entered. When he reached Shin's floor, his mom was standing at the door. She actually looked pleased to see him.

"Kevin, welcome. Thank you for joining us. Please do come in."

"It's good to see you again, Mrs. Tanaka. Thank you for inviting me."

Kevin tried to extend his right hand to shake hers, forgetting it was trapped in the sling. He pulled back, embarrassed he could not greet her properly.

"Please, Kevin," she said as she moved aside so he could enter. "It's okay. You're injured so we won't stand on that kind of formality this evening. How is your recovery?"

"Slow. I'll be in the sling for another four weeks or so. Writing with my left hand is tough. Some of my teachers are having a hard time reading my homework, so sometimes I have to read it back to them. But they are cool about it. Honestly, sometimes I have a hard time reading it, too!"

Kevin laughed nervously, and then felt a little stupid for making a joke.

"I'm glad your teachers are being considerate while you heal."

"Art is the most difficult. I can't draw right now. So my teacher wants me to explore what I can do with my left hand. He's super awesome, giving me different assignments from the rest of the class since I can't do the regular work."

As they entered the living room, Shin jumped up from one of the chairs and ran towards Kevin, wrapping him in a gentle hug. Shin's mom actually smiled and Shin had a giddy look Kevin hadn't seen in a while.

"It's awesome to see you," Shin said, letting Kevin go just as his father stood up from the couch.

Shin stood by Kevin as his father came around the couch to stand next to his wife.

"Kevin, welcome."

His father started to extend his hand, but then realized the sling. Kevin smiled on the inside since he'd made the same mistake just moments earlier. "Perhaps a different form of greeting will work better in this case." Mr. Tanaka bowed slightly at the waist. Kevin had seen enough movies to know he should do the same. He hoped his bow was adequate as to not give offense.

"Welcome to our home," Mr. Tanaka said. He sounded tense to Kevin, but without the anger from their first meeting. For all Kevin knew, this was his usual voice, or maybe, for some reason, he was nervous. "Please, let's sit."

Shin's parents returned to the couch. Kevin took the chair closest to him, between Shin and his father. When he sat he realized he was facing the couch, so he'd be addressing Shin's parents directly, which made him a little nervous.

"Before we go any further, Kevin, I must apologize for the way we treated you, especially me, when you were last here. Regardless of the circumstances, it was no way to treat a guest in our home and I hope you'll be able to forgive us so we can start again."

"I'd like that," Kevin said, measuring his words carefully. "Thank you for having me back. I really enjoyed discussing the artwork with Mrs. Tanaka the last time I was here."

"I enjoyed it as well. I'd like to show you more of our collection sometime. Would you like some tea before dinner?" she asked, lifting the teapot from the tray on the table.

"Yes, please. Thank you."

"Let me," Shin said, standing and taking the teapot from his mom. He set about preparing the tea.

"Thank you, Shin," his mother said as she sat back down.

"My wife and I have had many discussions over the past few

weeks, some including Shin. He told us he spoke to you and explained some of our beliefs and expectations. You need to know that I'm ashamed that our family was manipulated by an outsider to try and arrange a marriage to suit his own desires. While our family could benefit from joining to his, the way it was being handled was inappropriate. I apologize that you were pulled into such an unfortunate situation."

Mr. Tanaka adjusted his position and leaned forward on the couch, looking directly at Kevin. Kevin's father did the same thing when he was about to make an important point. The familiar gesture made him anxious. Shin was handing out cups of tea as his father continued.

"What directly affects you is our desire that our son date Japanese." Mr. Tanaka paused, for a long moment. Whether he was second guessing himself or simply trying to find the right words, Kevin couldn't tell. So he just waited, nodding his thanks to Shin when he received his tea.

"When Shin came out to us, we weren't thrilled," Mr. Tanaka finally continued. "It wasn't what we wanted for him. But, we're educated and know that being gay is part of his genetics. We love him, support him and do everything we can to make sure he's treated fairly by advocating for equality. While we've never discussed it, he's always brought home boys we thought were Japanese. But he's made it clear to us, in many ways, that you make him the happiest of any young man that he's met."

Kevin took a long sip from his tea, letting the warm, delicious flavor flow over his tongue. He wanted to steal a look at Shin to see how he was responding to all this, but felt he couldn't look away from Mr. Tanaka.

"I need to excuse myself," Mrs. Tanaka said, as she stood up. "I need to check on dinner. Please continue."

She circled behind the couch and disappeared down the hallway.

"It's difficult for us, and I'll admit, mostly for me, to change my expectations for my son. I did when he came out because I had to. It would've been unfair for me to force him to do something that was outside his control. Shin, and to a degree my wife, believe his love for you is the same. While I don't know that I subscribe to that completely, I also realize that I may be holding onto traditions that perhaps I should let go of."

"Dinner is ready," Mrs. Tanaka said from the doorway. "Shin, will you help me, please? Kevin, Junji, we'll join you in the dining room."

Shin hurried to join his mother in the kitchen while his father and Kevin entered the adjacent dining room. It was a comfortable space, with warm colors and bold artwork, dominated by a simple wooden table in the center. Shin's father gestured for him to take a seat. Kevin sat, his eyes taking in the paintings. He didn't recognize the artist nor could he read the signature, but he liked them very much.

"As I was saying," Mr. Tanaka continued, taking a seat as well, "dating Japanese may be a tradition we need to let go of. Shin said something that we've thought a lot about. If he has children, they may be adopted or conceived in a nontraditional way. That would be true whether he's with you or someone who is Japanese. In either case, the Tanaka name will continue, but the bloodline may not."

Shin and Mrs. Tanaka came in with food from the kitchen. Three platters were placed on the table. Kevin didn't recognize any of the dishes, but they smelled wonderful.

"Everything looks amazing, Mrs. Tanaka," Kevin said, as he placed a napkin in his lap.

"Thank you, Kevin. It looks more impressive than it really is, but I hope you like the taste."

"I'm sure I'll like them all."

"Before we eat, let me quickly finish with this part of the evening." Mr. Tanaka paused, taking a deep breath. "Shin is no longer grounded and is free to date you, and honestly to date anyone he chooses. When, and if, it comes time for marriage, we'll discuss what Shin's fiancé's intentions are."

Kevin had never seen Shin's father smile, until now. Shin and Mrs. Tanaka started to laugh, and Kevin joined them. All the awkwardness and anxious feeling evaporated. The nod to western culture made Kevin smile.

"Awesome, right, Kevin?" Shin said, grinning from across the table.

"Very," Kevin smiled back at Shin before returning his attention to Shin's father. "Thank you, Mr. Tanaka. I'm excited to go out with your son again. And thank you for sharing your side of things. It helps me understand better."

"Let's eat before everything gets cold," Mrs. Tanaka, said. "Kevin, please help yourself."

Kevin reached for one of the platters and had difficulty lifting it with his left hand because of its weight. Shin saw the trouble he was having.

"Let me help," he said, quickly coming around to Kevin's side of the table. Shin took Kevin's plate and filled it with a portion from each platter.

"Thanks." Kevin looked up at Shin and smiled again. Then he looked to the side of the plate and noticed the chopsticks. Very fine chopsticks. He'd never eaten in a home where chopsticks were the main utensils. "I'm sorry to have to ask this. Do you have a fork? I'm afraid I can't manage the chopsticks with my left hand."

"Oh, of course," Mrs. Tanaka, said. She started to stand, but Shin stopped her.

"I'll get it, mom, you and dad go ahead and get started." He went to the kitchen while his parents served themselves.

"He definitely likes you," Mrs. Tanaka said. "He's not usually this helpful at dinner."

She smiled and Kevin blushed as Shin returned with a fork and spoon so Kevin could choose whichever would work best.

"Thanks," Kevin said as Shin put the silverware on the table and went back to his seat.

Everyone began to eat. Kevin took small bites of each dish, savoring them individually.

"This is all amazing," Kevin said.

"I'm glad you like it," Mrs. Tanaka said.

"Can you tell me about these paintings?" Kevin asked, after eating in silence for a while. "I love the bright colors, but I don't recognize the artist."

Shin's parents recounted their discovery of the artist, who was based in Boston, and how they'd decided which of his works to acquire. Two of the pictures were reproductions, but they'd splurged on their twentieth anniversary for an original, which hung over the buffet sideboard.

After two hours of relaxed conversation, they finished their main courses and Shin's mom brought out a rich and creamy dessert. Like the dishes before it, it tasted wonderful. Kevin asked what it was called, but had a hard time with the pronunciation. Shin and his mother coached him until he had it right. Everyone smiled when he finally nailed it.

When dinner was over, Kevin said his goodnights to Mr. and Mrs. Tanaka in the living room before Shin walked him to the door.

"I love you," Shin whispered. "I'm looking forward to a ton of dates."

"Love you, too," Kevin said. "Hang out tomorrow?"

"As much as you want, yeah."

"Perfect. The rocks at eleven?"

"I'll be there."

They kissed briefly, before Kevin slipped out. He practically skipped all the way home.

SIXTEEN

"Man, I'm so psyched for you guys. Sounds like it went well last night," Marshall said as he and Kevin headed out of the brownstone.

"Yeah. It was a total reboot once Shin's dad explained everything. Crazy good food, great conversation. And I got a good night kiss, too."

Kevin knew he had a goofy grin on his face and he didn't care.

"Excellent. So now that you guys are back together all official, Cassie wants to know when we get to double. She asked about that last night after you texted me the good news. I don't know if that means she's already tired of me, or if she's into me enough that she just wants to add friends to the mix."

"Cassie's cool," Kevin said as they headed into Central Park. "So I bet it's the later. If we can hook D up with someone, maybe it could be a triple date. One of Cassie's friends maybe?"

"Couldn't hurt to ask. Maybe find out from Shin first if D would mind a blind date sort of thing?"

"I can... Hey, look who it is."

Shin was jogging up quickly to join them on the path.

"Perfect timing," Shin said as he greeted Kevin with a gentle hug. "Marshall, great to see you."

"You too, man." Marshall slapped Shin on the back. "Don't worry, I'm not going to hang around. I'm meeting up with the guys for pickup football. You two need time without a third wheel."

"You're so not a third wheel," Kevin said, as he took Shin's hand.

"Usually I'm not, but today is your first day officially back together."

"Always the wingman lookin' out for me," Kevin said. "Thanks." He gave Marshall a fist bump and then quickly got his hand back around Shin's.

"Catch you guys later," Marshall said as he took a fork in the path that led deeper into the park.

"See ya, Marshall," Shin called out. "So are you sure you want to watch me practice?"

"Yeah, man. And you haven't done it in a while either, being grounded and all. It's good for you to get back into it. And, maybe watching you will help me not forget all the moves."

"If only training worked just by watching," Shin winked at Kevin. "Let's see what I can do."

As they arrived at the rocks, Kevin plopped down on the ground and got as comfortable as he could. Meanwhile, Shin unslung his backpack and pulled out a t-shirt. He stripped off his sweatshirt and shoved it back into the pack. Kevin whistled while Shin stood before him shirtless.

"I've missed seeing that body. I dream about the afternoon in my bedroom when my mom almost caught us."

"Are you trying to make me blush?" Shin asked. "That's supposed to be *your* thing."

"I think it's working. I see just a hint of red."

"No you don't." Shin pulled the shirt over his head to hide his face, leaving his torso exposed.

"No fair. I like looking at your face as much as the rest of you." Shin slowly finished pulling the shirt on. "If it was warmer, I'd ask you to run without it."

"I'd think about going without it if you had your's off, too." He shot Kevin a sexy smile. "You're not the only one who has dreams, you know."

"We need to do that again. Soon. Very soon."

"Oh yeah we do." Shin stood still for a moment, and then he took off, hopping around doing his normal warmup. In a few minutes, Shin circled back to his usual starting place and took off on a routine Kevin knew. Shin was a little wobbly coming off the tree, but still nailed the landing, and he wasn't finished yet. He went from the landing into a one-handed handstand. Shin held the pose for a few seconds before dropping into a standing position.

"Where'd that come from? That was awesome, especially watching your abs flex trying to keep you balanced."

"I practiced at home, making sure I could hold the handstand. It works pretty well as an ending." Shin sat down next to Kevin and positioned himself so their legs touched. "Can I confess something?"

"Of course." Kevin was intrigued, and strangely not as concerned as he should be, considering recent events.

Shin looked out towards the rocks. "I haven't done a whole bunch of stuff with a guy before. What we did in your room that day was..."

Kevin put a finger to Shin's mouth to stop him. "You did just fine," he said, dragging his finger gently down Shin's lower lip. "And I don't care how much you've done or not done. I fooled around with my ex a fair bit, but nothing too serious. I'm just really glad you never got naked with Quan."

Shin shuddered at the thought. "Yeah. I'm not sure why I agreed to go out with him when he asked. He can be fun. His parents give him whatever he wants and let him go wherever, so we did some cool stuff. We kissed a few times, but he's not a good kisser. And with Yoon, I think we were too timid."

Kevin let go of Shin's hand, reached up and pulled his head closer. Their lips brushed, gently at first and then with more force as Kevin parted Shin's lips with his tongue. Shin pulled him closer and wrapped his lips around Kevin's tongue, allowing it to explore. He began to moan softly as Kevin drove deeper into his mouth. Shin reached up, running his hand along Kevin's arm and shoulder.

"That was kinda perfect," Kevin said when he pulled back.

"I thought so, too." Shin stared into Kevin's eyes. "Do you think people are watching us?"

"I don't care if they are. We can go back to my room if you want. The 'rents are out for a couple hours, at least."

Shin pulled back and stood up, offering Kevin a hand. "Not passing up that offer." Shin grabbed his pack and they were on their way, hand-in-hand.

"I'm glad we can start again," Shin said. "But I hate that we lost so much time, too."

"You realize you could discover something about me tomorrow that you don't like and we'll break up all over again."

"You could do the same," Shin said. "No matter what happens, I hope we can at least be friends because I think you're a cool guy."

"Agreed. Staying friends no matter what happens sounds good. One more thing, too."

"Um, okay." Shin sounded nervous.

"No more marriage talk until we're at least in our twenties."

Shin burst out laughing as they exited the park on Central Park West. "Definitely. I promise. No talk of marriage for at least six years." Shin cut his laughter short. "Oh, great. We need to start hanging in a part of town where we won't run in to him."

Quan approached and as soon as he saw the couple, he increased his speed. Kevin and Shin had stopped at the red light at CPW and 72nd since they needed to cross the street.

"I could text Marshall and see how fast he could get here to squash him."

Shin cracked up as Quan crossed 72nd Street. Kevin considered pulling them across CPW since the walk sign was in their favor, but Quan would have just followed. Better to get the altercation over with sooner rather than later.

"Oh sure, laugh it up," Quan said, sounding annoyed, as usual.

His hands were on his hips, and his body was tense. He looked like he was itching for another fight. "After what you did to me I ought to take you both down."

Shin and Kevin looked at each other and laughed again. Quan might connect with a punch on one of them, but he was no match for the two of them, even with Kevin only able to use one arm.

"Really?" Kevin said. "I think you're the one who did a number on us. It's one thing for his parents to want him to date Japanese, but for you to try and weasel yourself into marrying him was way out of line."

Quan glared at them while Shin and Kevin looked on in amusement. "Whatever, you both owe me. My parents are sending me to Japan for boarding school. They say I need discipline because I went behind their back talking to grandfather, meddling in affairs that were beneath me and disgracing our family."

Kevin was mixed on the response. It was great Quan was going away, but "affairs that were beneath me" was kind of insulting, maybe. He wasn't sure.

"Maybe you'll find your ideal man over there, someone who can put up with all your attitude," Shin said. "Or maybe the school will knock that crap out of you and turn you into someone pleasant to be around."

Quan seethed. He looked like he might pounce, but at the last second he pulled back, perhaps realizing that there was nothing to gain by starting a fight. It wouldn't change anything.

"Come on Kevin," Shin said, pulling on Kevin so they'd cross the street before the light changed.

Thankfully, Quan didn't follow. Kevin stole a quick glance back as they walked. Quan stared after them, his posture and expression declaring one thing. Defeat.

"Turns out we didn't need Marshall after all," Kevin said, planting a kiss on Shin's cheek as they reached the other side of the street.

Shin shrugged. "He's lucky I didn't punch him after all the shit he pulled." He laughed again. "Can you believe he thought he could take us down, really?"

Kevin thought about bringing up what happened with Quan at Fairway, but decided to save it for another time. He didn't want to spoil the moment.

Once they arrived at Kevin's apartment, they headed straight for his bedroom and closed the door behind them.

"Couple hours, huh?" Shin asked.

"Yeah." Kevin checked his watch.

"Cool."

Shin set his backpack on the floor and stepped up to Kevin. He put his hands on his waist and leaned in for a kiss, while making sure he didn't put pressure on Kevin's shoulder. As they kissed, Kevin ran his free hand under Shin's t-shirt and caressed his back.

"Can you please take your shirt off," Kevin asked between kisses.

Shin took a step back and pulled it over his head. "Better?"

"Very." Kevin smiled and felt up Shin's hard chest.

"What about you? Are you trapped in that shirt?"

"Nope. I've become an expert at getting in and out of shirts while making sure I don't piss off the shoulder."

Shin grinned and nodded, watching Kevin get out of the tee before putting the sling back in place.

"Come on," Kevin said, "let's lie back on the bed so that you can snuggle up next to me instead of bumping into the sling."

Kevin laid down near the wall so there was space for Shin and once he was settled, Shin laid down, making sure they were lined up to kiss. Kevin loved feeling Shin's bare skin against his.

After a few minutes Kevin gave a contented sigh between kisses.

"Everything okay?" Shin asked. "Comfortable enough?"

"Yeah. I'm doing great. I could stay like this for days, I think."

"Well, I can't wait for that sling to go so we don't have to worry about it anymore."

"I hear that."

"Can we go out tonight?" Shin asked.

"Absolutely. In fact, I'm supposed to ask you about maybe double dating with Marshall and Cassie, or even triple dating if we can set up D with someone."

"Can we can do that later? I'd really like for this weekend to be just us as much as possible."

Kevin nodded. "I'm for that. The others can wait a weekend, or even two." He stole more kisses. "I'm game for whatever you want to do."

"Right now, all I want is to kiss you all over." Shin planted a couple more kisses on Kevin's lips before he moved on to his neck and then down to his chest where he kissed all around the sling, and then some.

Kevin moaned softly with every touch of Shin's lips, loving how he worked his tongue over his skin.

Shin looked up at him and smiled. Kevin smiled back. He felt so lucky that Shin was back in his life, and while it sucked being hurt, he knew everything from here on out was going to be perfect.

ACKNOWLEDGMENTS

There's a small team of awesome people who help me get my books out and I can't thank them enough. Will Knauss, my husband, is a great sounding board, cheerleader, inspiration, reader and, when he needs to be, task master. Elvis Murks is an indispensable beta reader. Connor Youngberg and Gareth Cj. Wee also provided valuable guidance for this book.

I'm tremendously grateful to the readers who pick up my books and I love that the stories I tell have found an audience. I hope you enjoy the story of Kevin and Shin as well. Please tell me what you think of this (or any of my books), by writing reviews and/or contracting me through my website at jeffadamswrites.com.

YOUNG ADULT BOOKS BY JEFF ADAMS

Each of these titles are available in ebook, paperback and audiobook

Codename: Winger series

Tracker Hacker (includes the bonus short story *A Very Winger Christmas*)

Schooled

Audio Assault

Netminder

Other Young Adult Titles

Flipping for Him

ABOUT THE AUTHOR

Jeff Adams has written stories since he was in middle school and became a published author in 2009 when his first short stories were published. He writes both gay romance and LGBTQ+ young adult fiction...and there's usually a hockey player at the center of the story.

Jeff lives in central California with his husband of more than twenty years, Will. Some of his favorite things include the musicals *Rent* and *[title of show]*, the Detroit Red Wings and Pittsburgh Penguins hockey teams, and the reality TV competition *So You Think You Can Dance*. He, of course, loves to read, but there isn't enough space to list out his favorite books.

Jeff and Will are also podcasters. The *Big Gay Fiction Podcast* is a weekly show devoted to gay romance as well as pop culture. New episodes come out every Monday at BigGayFictionPodcast.com.

Learn more about Jeff, his books and find his social media links at JeffAdamsWrites.com.

Made in the USA
Las Vegas, NV
06 June 2021

24267645R00075